模擬測驗完整解析

● 確認正確答案後，務必仔細閱讀「完整解析」，徹底通透問題點。
● 無法聽懂的內容，務必翻覆聆聽直到理解為止。
● 模擬測驗以美、英、澳、加四國口音錄製，分別以   標示。
● 每道題目錄製成一軌，方便重覆聆聽。

Test 1 完整解析

Part ①

1. 答案：(C)

美

圖 析 有兩個人對坐，正在玩桌上的西洋象棋。

解 析 本題的重點在考「受詞」。四個選項中的動詞皆為 playing，而 (A) baseball、(B) music 和 (D) cards 三個選項中的受詞皆與照片不符，故 (C) chess 為正確答案。

錄音內容 (A) They're playing baseball.
(B) They're playing music.
(C) They're playing chess.
(D) They're playing cards.

錄音翻譯 (A) 他們在打棒球。
(B) 他們在放音樂。
(C) 他們在下棋。
(D) 他們在打牌。

☐ play chess 玩西洋象棋

2. 答案：(D)

加

圖 析 計程車旁站著一位女子，她前面有兩個行李箱，左邊及背景有一些路人。

解 析 本題的關鍵字為 woman、standing、next to、taxi。(A) 錯在沒有人在 moving luggage；(B) 錯在沒人在 checking out，而地點 front desk 也不對；(C) 錯在地點 outdoor café；故答案為 (D)。

錄音內容 (A) The men are moving some heavy luggage.
(B) Some people are checking out at the front desk.
(C) There are some people in an outdoor café.
(D) There is a woman standing next to a taxi.

錄音翻譯 (A) 男子們在搬一些重的行李。
(B) 有些人在櫃台辦理退房。
(C) 戶外的咖啡廳有一些人。
(D) 有位女子站在計程車旁邊。

☐ luggage [ˋlʌgɪdʒ] *n.*【英】行李　　☐ outdoor [ˋaʊtˏdor] *adj.* 戶外的
☐ check out 結帳離開　　☐ next to 緊鄰著
☐ front desk 櫃臺

Test 1

Part
1

Part
2

Part
3

Part
4

Test 2

Part
1

Part
2

Part
3

Part
4

簡

答

3. 答案：(A)　　　　　　　　　　　　　　　　　　　　　　英

> 圖 析　一位女子在路邊看報紙，手上拿著包包，背景有車經過，左前方有一些人。
>
> 解 析　本題關鍵字為 woman、reading。(B) 錯在動詞 buying；(C) 錯在動詞 sitting；(D) 錯在動詞 getting 及地點 library；故答案應選 (A)。

錄音內容　(A) The woman is reading.
　　　　　(B) The woman is buying a newspaper.
　　　　　(C) The woman is sitting.
　　　　　(D) The woman is getting a book at the library.

錄音翻譯　(A) 這位女子在看書。
　　　　　(B) 這位女子在買報紙。
　　　　　(C) 這位女子坐著。
　　　　　(D) 這位女子在圖書館借書。

☐ library [ˈlaɪˌbrɛrɪ] *n.* 圖書館

4. 答案：(C)　　　　　　　　　　　　　　　　　　　　　　澳

> 圖 析　一群人在月臺內準備上車，左邊的女子回頭，右邊的男人有披圍巾。
>
> 解 析　本題選項的主詞皆同，故關鍵要聽「動作」。(A) 的 training（訓練）為相似音陷阱，文不對題；(B) 的 elevator（電梯）和 (D) 的 escalator（手扶梯）皆與照片不符，故答案應選 (C)。

錄音內容　(A) People are getting some training.
　　　　　(B) People are taking an elevator.
　　　　　(C) People are getting on a subway.
　　　　　(D) People are taking an escalator.

錄音翻譯　(A) 大家在接受一些訓練。
　　　　　(B) 大家在搭電梯。
　　　　　(C) 大家在搭地鐵。
　　　　　(D) 大家在搭電扶梯。

☐ training [ˈtrenɪŋ] *n.* 訓練　　　　☐ escalator [ˈɛskəˌletə] *n.* 電扶梯

5. 答案：(D)

美

圖 析 一位女子正在吃手上的蘋果。

解 析 本題考動詞與受詞的誤用。(A) 錯在 cutting；(B) 錯在受詞 applesauce（蘋果醬）；(C) 錯在動詞 picking；(D) 關鍵字為 taking、bite、apple 皆與照片吻合，故為正確答案。

錄音內容 (A) The woman is cutting an apple.
(B) The woman is eating applesauce.
(C) The woman is picking apples.
(D) The woman is taking a bite of an apple.

錄音翻譯 (A) 這位女士在切蘋果。
(B) 這位女士在吃蘋果醬。
(C) 這位女士在採蘋果。
(D) 這位女士在咬一口蘋果。

☐ applesauce [ˈæplˌsɔs] *n.* 蘋果醬　　　☐ bite [baɪt] *n.* 一口的量

6. 答案：(A)

加

圖 析 一男一女正在檢查車子的輪胎，男子是蹲著，女子是站著。

解 析 本題考「受詞」誤用。(A) 關鍵字為 checking、car tire 與照片相符，故為正確答案。(B) 的 time 和 (C) 的 luggage 及 (D) 的 room 皆為錯誤受詞，故不可選。

錄音內容 (A) They're checking the car tire.
(B) They're checking the time.
(C) They're checking their luggage.
(D) They're checking out of their room.

錄音翻譯 (A) 他們在檢查車胎。
(B) 他們在查看時間。
(C) 他們在檢查行李。
(D) 他們在辦退房。

Test 1

Part

1

Part

2

Part

3

Part

4

Test 2

Part

1

Part

2

Part

3

Part

4

簡

答

7. 答案：(C)   英

> 圖 析 有一把鑰匙插在門鎖裡。

> 解 析 本題考介系詞片語的誤用。(A) on the shelf、(B) in the drawer 和 (D) on the table 皆與照片不符，(C) in the lock 與圖片一致，故為正確答案。

> 錄音內容 (A) The key is on the shelf.
> (B) The keys are in the drawer.
> (C) The key is in the lock.
> (D) The keys are on the table.

> 錄音翻譯 (A) 鑰匙在架子上。
> (B) 鑰匙在抽屜裡。
> (C) 鑰匙在門鎖裡。
> (D) 鑰匙在桌子上。

> □ shelf [ʃɛlf] *n.* 架子   □ lock [lɑk] *n.* 鎖
> □ drawer [ˋdrɔə] *n.* 抽屜

8. 答案：(B)   澳

> 圖 析 一位戴帽子的警官站在路障前，身上掛有 police 的標幟，身後有幾個路人。

> 解 析 本題重點在考動詞和受詞的誤用。(A) 錯在警官並沒有 getting out of a car；(C) 錯在 leaning 的受詞 car；(D) 錯在 standing on his hands（倒立）。(B) 動詞 wearing 及受詞 hat 皆正確，故為正確選項。

> 錄音內容 (A) The officer is getting out of a car.
> (B) The officer is wearing a hat.
> (C) The officer is leaning on his car.
> (D) The officer is standing on his hands.

> 錄音翻譯 (A) 這位警官在下車。
> (B) 這位警官戴著帽子。
> (C) 這位警官靠在他的車子上。
> (D) 這位警官在倒立。

> □ get out of 自……出來   □ stand on one's hands 倒立
> □ lean on 倚靠

9. 答案：(D)

美

圖 析 一個女子的手正握著桌上茶杯的把手。

解 析 本題選項主詞皆相同，重點在考動詞及受詞錯誤。(A) 動詞 filling 有誤；(B) 動詞 washing 有誤，sink 也不對；(C) 動詞 pouring 有誤。(D) 的關鍵字為 holding、cup 及 handle 皆與圖片相符，故為正確答案。

錄音內容 (A) She's filling the cup with coffee.
(B) She's washing the cup in the sink.
(C) She's pouring water into the cup.
(D) She's holding the cup by the handle.

錄音翻譯 (A) 她正把杯子倒滿咖啡。
(B) 她正在水槽裡洗杯子。
(C) 她正把水倒進杯子裡。
(D) 她正握住杯子的把手。

- [ ] fill A with B 以 B 注滿 A
- [ ] sink [sɪŋk] *n.* 水槽
- [ ] pour [por] *v.* 灌；注
- [ ] handle [ˋhændl] *n.* 把手

10. 答案：(B)

加

圖 析 一架飛機停在登機門旁。

解 析 本題選項主詞皆同，重點在動詞或介系詞片語。(A) 錯在動詞 landing；(C) 錯在動詞 taking off；(D) 錯在動詞 flying；故應選 (B)。

錄音內容 (A) The airplane is landing.
(B) The airplane is at the gate.
(C) The airplane is taking off.
(D) The airplane is flying over the city.

錄音翻譯 (A) 這架飛機正在降落。
(B) 這架飛機在登機門旁。
(C) 這架飛機正在起飛。
(D) 這架飛機正飛越這座城市。

- [ ] land [lænd] *v.* 降落
- [ ] gate [get] *n.* 登機門
- [ ] take off 起飛

Part 2

11. 答案：(A)

加 ▶ 英

破 題 How/much/is/jacket? ⇨ 問「價錢」。

解 析 題目問夾克價格，故表價錢的 (A) seventy dollars 為正確答案。(B) 原句主詞 that jacket 為單數，故主詞 they 不對。(C) 題目並非問顏色，答非所問。

錄音內容 How much is that jacket?
(A) It's seventy dollars.
(B) They are out of my size.
(C) It comes in gray and navy blue.

錄音翻譯 那件外套多少錢？
(A) 七十美元。
(B) 已經沒有我的尺寸了。
(C) 有灰色和深藍色的。

☐ be out of one's size 沒有某人的尺寸   ☐ navy blue 深藍色

12. 答案：(C)

美 ▶ 英

破 題 When/I/need/turn timesheet in? ⇨ 問「時間」。

解 析 以問表「時間」的 When 起頭，故應選有時間字眼的 (C) by Friday。(A) 不對，因以 Wh 開頭的問句，不可用 Yes 或 No 回答。(B) 也錯，原句主詞為 I，故回答不可能用 I，且回答中用 time 來混淆題目中的 timesheet。

錄音內容 When do I need to turn my timesheet in?
(A) Yes, to Jenny at the front desk.
(B) I know, and it's about time, too.
(C) You'll need to get it in by Friday.

錄音翻譯 我的工時表需要在什麼時候交？
(A) 對，交給櫃檯的珍妮。
(B) 我知道，而且時候也到了。
(C) 你要在星期五以前交來。

☐ turn in 交出 (= submit [səbˋmɪt])   ☐ front desk 櫃臺
☐ timesheet 時間表

13. 答案：(A)

澳▶英

破題 Where/can/I/park/car? ⇨ 問「地點」。

解析 以問「地點」的 Where 開頭，故 (A) in the lot 為正確答案。(B) 為「一字多義」陷阱，題目中的 park 為動詞「停車」，而答案中的 park（公園）則為名詞。(C) 答非所問，因 four dollars 指「金額」。

錄音內容 Where can I park my car?

(A) In the lot behind the building.

(B) It's a nice park with lots of trees.

(C) It costs four dollars per hour.

錄音翻譯 我可以把車停在哪裡？

(A) 停在大樓後面的空地上。

(B) 那是座有很多樹不錯的公園。

(C) 每小時要價四美元。

☐ park [pɑrk] *v.* 停車　　　　　　☐ lot [lɑt] *n.* （做特定用途的）一塊地

14. 答案：(A)

英▶加

破題 Could/you/show/Donna/where...? ⇨ 問「可否」告知。

解析 (A) 以 Sure 表肯定，且後面的 take her there 也回應了問題重點。(B) 錯在「主客易位」，問題重點是在帶 Donna 去看 Mr. Lang 的辦公室，因此 Mr. Lang 非重點。(C) 文不對題，office 並非問題重點。

錄音內容 Could you show Donna where Mr. Lang's office is?

(A) Sure, I'll take her there myself.

(B) Hello, Mr. Lang, it's nice to meet you.

(C) A corner office with a nice view.

錄音翻譯 你能不能告訴多娜郎先生的辦公室在哪裡？

(A) 好啊，我會自己帶她去。

(B) 哈囉，郎先生，幸會。

(C) 視野不錯的角落辦公室。

☐ view [vju] *n.* 視野

15. 答案：(B)

澳▶美

破 題 How long/will/it/take...? ⇨ 問「要花多少時間」。

解 析 (A) 答非所問，Because 表「原因」。(C) 亦答非所問，quicker 表「比較」的概念，與問題無關。(B) estimating two years 可呼應問題重點，故為正確答案。注意，問題中的 it 為虛主詞，表 to repair the bridge。

錄音內容 How long will it take them to repair the bridge?
(A) Because it's a hundred years old.
(B) They're estimating two years.
(C) It's quicker to go that way.

錄音翻譯 他們要多久才能把橋修好？
(A) 因為它有一百年之久。
(B) 他們估計要兩年。
(C) 走那條路比較快。

☐ repair [rɪˋpɛr] v. 修理   ☐ estimate [ˋɛstə‚met] v. 估計

16. 答案：(B)

澳▶加

破 題 Can you/show me/reports? ⇨ 問「是否」能給我看報告。

解 析 (A) 不對，Thanks 應為提問者之後的回覆；(C) 錯在「重點轉移」，因為 fifty pages 非問題重點。(B) 開頭的 Sure，對應了題目重點 Can you...?，答句中主詞 I 及介系詞 for 的受詞 you 也完全呼應題目的主詞 you 及受詞 me，而後面的回答亦呼應了問題重點。

錄音內容 Can you show me some sample reports?
(A) Thanks, I'll read them today.
(B) Sure, I'll print one out for you.
(C) About fifty pages, including the tables and graphs.

錄音翻譯 你能給我看一些樣本報告嗎？
(A) 謝謝，我今天就會看。
(B) 好啊，我印一份出來給你。
(C) 差不多五十頁，包括表格和圖表。

☐ print out 列印   ☐ graph [græf] n. 圖表
☐ table [ˋtebl] n. 表格

17. 答案：(A)

加 ▶ 澳

破題 Are/cookies/us/eat? ⇨ 問餅乾「是否」是給我們吃的。

解析 (A) Yes 回答了問句，且 they 代表問題中的 cookies，故為正確答案。left over 表「剩下」之意。(B) No, thanks 答非所問，且原問句重點為 us 而非 I，而 hungry 是題目重點字 eat 的聯想陷阱。(C) 答非所問，題目是問「是否」可吃，而非「食物」名稱。

錄音內容 Are those cookies for us to eat?
(A) Yes, they're left over from the staff meeting.
(B) No thanks, I'm not hungry.
(C) Chocolate chip and sugar cookies.

錄音翻譯 那些餅乾是要給我們吃的嗎？
(A) 是的，那是員工大會剩下的。
(B) 不用了，謝謝，我不餓。
(C) 巧克力片和糖餅乾。

☐ be left over from 從……剩下的　　☐ staff meeting 員工會議

18. 答案：(C)

加 ▶ 美

破題 Who's/meeting/Mr. Park/airport? ⇨ 問「誰」會去接機。

解析 (A) 用 When 疑問句回答，不能呼應題目重點。(B) 聽到 airport，出現 flight 為「聯想陷阱」，因 flight 並非問句重點。(C) 以 John 回應 Who，助動詞 would 則代表了問句中的 meet，故為正確答案。

錄音內容 Who's meeting Mr. Park at the airport?
(A) When does your flight arrive?
(B) It's a direct flight from Paris.
(C) John said he would.

錄音翻譯 誰會去機場接朴先生？
(A) 你的班機什麼時候會到？
(B) 它是從巴黎出發的直達班機。
(C) 約翰說他會去。

☐ meet [mit] v. 迎接　　　　　　　　☐ flight [flaɪt] n.（飛機的）班次；飛機的
☐ direct flight 直達班機　　　　　　　　航程

19. 答案：(B)   英▶美

破 題 Did/Aaron Price/leave/his address? ⇨ 問「是否」留下住址。

解 析 (A) 動詞 buy 文不對題。(C) 答非所問，worked here 沒有呼應題目重點。
(B) Yes 回應了問題，且 gave business card 就等於是 leave his address。

錄音內容 Did Aaron Price leave his address?
(A) Yes, but he said he would just buy a new one.
(B) Yes, he gave me his business card.
(C) He worked here three years ago.

錄音翻譯 艾倫‧普萊斯有沒有留下他的地址？
(A) 有，可是他說他會直接買個新的。
(B) 有，他給了我他的名片。
(C) 他三年前在這裡工作。

☐ business card 名片

20. 答案：(B)   加▶美

破 題 What incentive/can/you/give/them? ⇨ 問可提供「什麼」誘因。

解 析 (A) 答非所問，用 Okay 開頭即不合句意。(C) Probably 為「不確定」的
字眼，亦未回答題目重點。(B) We 呼應了題目之 you，而 offer a twenty-
percent discount 即題目所問的重點：incentive。

錄音內容 What incentive can you give them?
(A) Okay, I'll be sure to do that.
(B) We can offer a twenty-percent discount on the first order.
(C) Probably, but we'll have to talk about it.

錄音翻譯 你們能給他們什麼誘因？
(A) 好，我一定會這麼做。
(B) 第一筆訂單我們可以打八折。
(C) 大概吧，不過我們必須討論它。

☐ incentive [ɪnˋsɛntɪv] *n.* 誘因   ☐ discount [ˋdɪskaʊnt] *n.* 折扣

21. 答案：(A)

加 ▶ 美

破題 Did you enjoy the movie? ⇨ 問「是否」喜愛電影。

解析 (A) It 指 the movie，而 better than I expected 即等於「喜歡」，故為正確答案。(B) 答非所問，saw it 為聯想陷阱。(C) 的 at eight 強調時間，則文不對題。

錄音內容 Did you enjoy the movie?
(A) It was much better than I expected.
(B) I saw it last week with my brother.
(C) It starts at eight, I think.

錄音翻譯 你喜歡這部電影嗎？
(A) 它比我預期的好多了。
(B) 我是上星期和我弟弟一起看的。
(C) 我想它是八點開演。

22. 答案：(C)

澳 ▶ 美

破題 How/you/know/where/find me? ⇨ 問找我的「方法」。

解析 (A) 受詞 it 錯誤，而 desk 的指「地方」亦不符合問題重點。(B) 原句中受詞為 me，故此處受詞 him 為錯誤，且用 known 故意混淆問句中的 know。(C) office number 為找到人的線索，而 listed dowstairs 為線索所在，故為正確答案。

錄音內容 How did you know where to find me?
(A) I found it on your desk.
(B) I've known him since we were in college together.
(C) Your office number is listed downstairs.

錄音翻譯 你怎麼知道要去哪裡找我？
(A) 我是在你的桌上找到的。
(B) 打從我們一起讀大學時，我就認識他了。
(C) 你的辦公室號碼就列在樓下。

23. 答案：(B)

破 題 Are we supposed/make presentation? ⇨ 問「是否」要做簡報。

解 析 (A) 主詞 It 錯誤。(C)「重點轉移」，題目問 we，用 their presentation 回答有誤。本題應選 (B)，An informal one 指「一個非正式的報告」，one 即指 presentation。

錄音內容 Are we supposed to make a presentation at the meeting?
(A) It's supposed to be, but I don't think it is.
(B) An informal one, just so people know what we're working on.
(C) I thought their presentation was one of the better ones.

錄音翻譯 我們應該在開會時提出報告嗎？
(A) 應該要是，不過我想它並不是。
(B) 非正式的報告，只是要讓大家知道我們在做什麼。
(C) 我想他們的報告是其中比較好的一個。

- ☐ make a presentation 做簡報
- ☐ be supposed to do 應該做……
- ☐ informal [ɪnˋfɔrml] *adj.* 非正式的
- ☐ work on sth. 正在處理某事

24. 答案：(C)

破 題 Your car/broke down/again? ⇨ 直述句形式的問句，用來「確認」對方所說的話。

解 析 (A) 答非所問，last one 與主題無關。(B) 中的 keyboard 為「無中生有」。(C) 的 Yes 呼應問題，而 time to replace it 呼應 broke down again，故為正確答案。

錄音內容 Your car broke down again?
(A) No, this is the last one.
(B) It needs a new keyboard.
(C) Yes, I think it's time to replace it.

錄音翻譯 你的車又拋錨了嗎？
(A) 沒有，這是最後一個。
(B) 它需要一個新鍵盤。
(C) 是啊，我想是該把它換掉了。

- ☐ break down 故障
- ☐ keyboard [ˋkibord] *n.* 鍵盤
- ☐ replace [rɪˋples] *v.* 替換

25. 答案：(C)

澳▶美

破 題 Has/Riley/provided/feedback ⇨ 問「是否」提提供回饋。

解 析 (A)「主客易位」，proposal 並非問題的主詞。(B) 語意不清，notice that 並未指出是否 provided feedback。本題應選 (C)，would e-mail his comments 表示他會提供意見。

錄音內容 Has Riley provided us with any feedback on our proposal yet?

(A) It's a proposal to supply the city with new traffic lights.

(B) Yes, I've noticed that as well.

(C) He said he would e-mail his comments this afternoon.

錄音翻譯 對於我們的提案，萊里給了什麼意見沒有？

(A) 那是要為城市裝設新紅綠燈的提案。

(B) 有，我也注意到了那點。

(C) 他說他今天下午會用電子郵件把他的意見寄來。

☐ provide A with B (= provide B for A)
提供 B 給 A
☐ feedback [ˋfidˏbæk] *n.* 反饋（的信息）
☐ proposal [prəˋpozl] *n.* 提案

☐ traffic light 紅綠燈
☐ as well 也；同樣地
☐ comment [ˋkamɛnt] *n.* 意見；評論

26. 答案：(B)

英▶澳

破 題 Do you know when...? ⇨ 插入句，重點在後面問「時間」的 when。

解 析 (A) 不對，問題重點在 when，不應用 Yes 或 No 回答。(C) 重覆題目字 know 與 open，但問句並未問原因，不能用 because 回答。本題應選 (B)，open at seven 回應了重點。

錄音內容 Do you know when the copy center downstairs opens?

(A) Yes, I need three hundred copies.

(B) I think it opens at seven.

(C) I know. I opened it because it was too hot in here.

錄音翻譯 你知道樓下的影印中心何時開門營業嗎？

(A) 對，我需要三百份。

(B) 我想是七點開門。

(C) 我知道，我把它打開是因為這裡面太熱了。

☐ copy [ˋkapɪ] *n.* 副本；拷貝

27. 答案：(B)

破 題 can you tell me where...? ⇨ 重點在後面「插入句」的 where，問「地方」。

解 析 (A) 重點轉移，原句重點在 nearest bus stop 之處，而不在 fare（票價）。(C) 直接跳過題目重點而回答 get off at... stop，為聯想陷阱。(B) 中的 go、turn、see 皆為指引「方向」的指標字眼，故為正確答案。

錄音內容 Excuse me, can you tell me where the nearest bus stop for bus number ten is?
(A) Yes, the fare has gone up twenty percent in the past three years.
(B) Yes, go to the corner, turn left, and you'll see it about halfway down the block.
(C) No, you have to get off at the last stop.

錄音翻譯 對不起，你可不可以告訴我十路公車最近的公車站在哪裡？
(A) 對，票價在過去三年內漲了兩成。
(B) 好的，到轉角左轉，大約走到街區一半左右的時候，你就會看到。
(C) 不行，你必須在最後一站下車。

□ bus stop 公車的停車站
□ fare [fɛr] *n.* 票價
□ halfway [ˋhæf͵we] *adv.* 在中途
□ get off 下車

28. 答案：(A)

破 題 Which/database programs/you/used? ⇨ Wh 問句，問使用過「何種」軟體。

解 析 (A) familiar 及 DataMaster 呼應了問題重點，為正確答案。(B) 與 (C) 犯了一樣的錯誤：Wh 開頭的問句，不應用 Yes 或 No 回答。

錄音內容 Which database programs have you used?
(A) I'm only familiar with DataMaster.
(B) Yes, I got a used one on sale.
(C) No, but I'm probably going to learn to.

錄音翻譯 你用過哪些資料庫程式？
(A) 我只熟悉資料大師。
(B) 對，我拍賣的時候買了一個舊的。
(C) 沒有，不過我大概會去學。

□ be familiar with sth. 熟悉某事
□ used [ˋjuzd] *adj.* 舊的；二手的
□ on sale 拍賣中

29. 答案：(B)

英▶美

破 題 Why don't we...? ⇨ 表提供「建議」，回答者應針對建議回應。

解 析 (A) 重覆題目用字 work、while 故弄玄虛，且答非所問。(C) 文不對題，題目並非問「位置」。(B) I think that's a good idea. 表接受對方意見，故為正解。

錄音內容 Why don't we put this aside and work on something else for a while?

(A) Yes, I worked there for a while in the late nineties.

(B) Yes, I think that's a good idea.

(C) I think I put it on my desk.

錄音翻譯 我們為什麼不把這擺在一邊，暫時先做別的事？

(A) 對，我九〇年代末期在那裡服務過一陣子。

(B) 對，我想那是個好主意。

(C) 我想我把它放在我桌上了。

☐ put sth. aside 把某事擱在一旁　　☐ for a while 一會兒

30. 答案：(B)

澳▶英

破 題 Where/decide/go/vacation? ⇨ 要去「何處」度假。

解 析 (A) 答非所問，for + 時間表「時間長度」。(C) 不對，因為用 Wh 開頭的問句，不用 Yes 或 No 回答。(B) I、visit、New York 表明了「說話者要去的地點」，故為正確答案。

錄音內容 Where did you decide to go on your vacation?

(A) For two weeks in July.

(B) I'm going to visit my cousin in New York.

(C) Yes, that was the decision management made.

錄音翻譯 你決定休假時要去哪裡？

(A) 七月時去兩個星期。

(B) 我會去紐約看我表弟。

(C) 對，那就是管理階層的決定。

☐ management [ˋmænɪdʒmənt] *n.* 管理階層

Test 1

Part
1

Part
2

Part
3

Part
4

Test 2

Part
1

Part
2

Part
3

Part
4

簡

答

31. 答案：(C)

加▶澳

破題 If/blue tag/fifty percent off? ⇨ 考「直述句」，必須了解說話者的「意圖」，才能正確作答。

解析 題目表示在「某種限制」情況下有打折的好處。(A) 語意不清，like... better 是用在兩者之間的比較；(B) 答非所問，題目並非討論數量；(C) 為感嘆句，表示對事情的看法，而 What a good deal!（真划算！）則回應了題目中所提到的好處。

錄音內容 If it has a blue tag, it's fifty percent off.
(A) I think I liked the green one better.
(B) Fifty or sixty of them, I think.
(C) What a good deal!

錄音翻譯 假如有藍標的話，就是打五折。
(A) 我想我比較喜歡綠色的。
(B) 我想有五、六十個。
(C) 真是划算！

☐ tag [tæg] *n.* 標籤　　☐ good deal 好價錢；好買賣 (= real bargain)

32. 答案：(A)

英▶澳

破題 Was it crowded...? ⇨ 問「是否」會很擁擠。

解析 (A) 用 No 對應了 Was 問句，且 not too bad 也回應了問題，表示不會 crowded，為正確選項。(B) 答非所問，題目並未問原因，因此不用 Because 回答。(C) 主詞 I 不正確，題目問的是銀行。

錄音內容 Was it crowded at the bank?
(A) No, not too bad.
(B) Because I was opening a new account.
(C) Yes, I was the only one who was there.

錄音翻譯 銀行裡很擠嗎？
(A) 不，還不算太糟。
(B) 因為我在開新帳戶。
(C) 對，只有我一個人在那裡。

☐ crowded [ˋkraʊdɪd] *adj.* 擁擠的　　☐ open an account 開立帳戶

33. 答案：(A)

澳 ▶ 加

破 題 many/applicants/hard to/decision ⇨「直述句」，表示人選太多很難決定。

解 析 (A) 表示回答者瞭解狀況也同意說話者的看法，為正確答案。(B) red 為「無中生有」，與題目無關。(C) apply（申請）為相關字陷阱，混淆題目用字 applicants（申請人），實則答非所問。

錄音內容 There are so many qualified applicants, it's hard to make a decision.
(A) I know, they're all very good.
(B) I suggest the red one, it's cheaper.
(C) Maybe you can apply online.

錄音翻譯 有這麼多合格的申請人，令人難以決定。
(A) 我知道，他們都很優秀。
(B) 我建議紅色的，它比較便宜。
(C) 也許你可以上網申請。

□ qualified [ˈkwɑlə.faɪd] *adj.* 合格的　　□ apply [əˈplaɪ] *v.* 申請
□ applicant [ˈæpləkənt] *n.* 申請人　　□ make a decision　作決定

34. 答案：(C)

澳 ▶ 加

破 題 There isn't..., is there? ⇨「附加問句」，回答者應表示「有或沒有」。

解 析 (A) 不對，主詞不該用 I 回應；(B) 重覆重點字 flight 混淆作答，文不對題；故本題應選 (C)。

錄音內容 There isn't an earlier flight, is there?
(A) I'd try to get there a little early if I were you.
(B) No, my flight got in early.
(C) I'm afraid that's the earliest.

錄音翻譯 沒有比較早的班機了，有嗎？
(A) 假如我是你的話，我會試著早一點到那裡去。
(B) 不，我的班機早到了。
(C) 恐怕那是最早的了。

□ get in　到達

Test 1

Part 1
Part 2
Part 3
Part 4
Test 2
Part 1
Part 2
Part 3
Part 4
簡答

35. 答案：(C)

加▶英

破題 Are/we/out of...? ⇨ 問「是否」用完某樣東西，要回答 Yes 或 No。

解析 (A) 不對，原句沒問原因，不該用 Because 回答。(B) 文不對題，原句根本沒有提到 he。(C) some on bottom shelf 回應了問題重點，表示並未用完，故為正確答案。

錄音內容 Are we out of the large envelopes?
(A) Because the others weren't big enough.
(B) He's out of the office today.
(C) There should be some on the bottom shelf.

錄音翻譯 我們的大信封用完了嗎？
(A) 因為其他的不夠大。
(B) 他今天不在辦公室。
(C) 架子最底下應該有一些。

☐ out of sth. 用完某物　　　☐ bottom [ˋbɑtəm] *n.* 底部；下端

36. 答案：(B)

英▶加

破題 How/photo/look/here? ⇨ 問照片看起來「如何」。

解析 (A) 答非所問，問 photo，提到 camera 為「聯想陷阱」。(C) 文不對題，題目並沒有提到照片的內容或主題。(B) I think it's too big... 表「看法」，呼應了問題重點，為正確答案。

錄音內容 How does this photo look here?
(A) With my new digital camera.
(B) I think it's too big for that space.
(C) Mostly photos of my friends and family.

錄音翻譯 這張照片擺這裡看起來怎麼樣？
(A) 用我的新數位相機。
(B) 我想放在那個地方顯得太大了。
(C) 大多是我親友的照片。

☐ mostly [ˋmostlɪ] *adv.* 大部分　　　☐ digital [ˋdɪdʒɪtl] *adj.* 數位的

37. 答案：(A)   英▶美

破 題 Shouldn't we...? ⇨ 表提出建議，應回答「接受或不接受」此建議。

解 析 (A) Yes, I think... should. 充分回答了問題的重點，為正解。(B) 人稱錯誤，he 應改為 we。(C) 人稱錯誤，they 應改為 we。

錄音內容 Shouldn't we ask Greg for help on the MacArthur project?
(A) Yes, I think we probably should.
(B) No, I don't think he should.
(C) I'm not sure whether they would.

錄音翻譯 我們在麥克阿瑟計畫上不應該請葛雷幫忙嗎？
(A) 應該，我想我們或許該這麼做。
(B) 不應該，我認為他不該這麼做。
(C) 我不確定他們願不願意。

☐ **ask sb. for help** 請某人給予協助

38. 答案：(C)   澳▶美

破 題 Can/you/ship/order? ⇨ 問「可不可以」運送訂貨。

解 析 (A) 答非所問。注意，order 在此為動詞，而原問句 order 為名詞。(B) 不知所云。(C) We、should、able、ship 呼應了問句重點，故為正確答案。

錄音內容 Can you ship our order this week?
(A) I ordered mine a week ago.
(B) I'm afraid that's not what we ordered.
(C) We should be able to ship it by Wednesday.

錄音翻譯 你們可不可以這星期運送我們的訂貨？
(A) 我在一星期前訂了我的東西。
(B) 恐怕那不是我們訂的東西。
(C) 我們應該可以在星期三前運送。

☐ **ship** [ʃɪp] *v.* 運送   ☐ **order** [ˋɔrdɚ] *n.* 訂單 / *v.* 訂（貨）

39. 答案：(A)

破 題 Where/get/hair cut? ⇨ 問「地點」。

解 析 (A) go to... Salon 回應了題目重點，故為正解。(B) 與 (C) 皆錯，因為 Wh 問句不用 Yes 或 No 來回答。

錄音內容 Where do you get your hair cut?
(A) I go to Maxi Cut Salon.
(B) Yes, I'm getting it cut tomorrow.
(C) No, I'm letting my hair grow.

錄音翻譯 你在哪裡剪頭髮？
(A) 我在馬西髮廊剪。
(B) 對，我明天要剪。
(C) 不，我要留頭髮。

□ get one's hair cut 剪頭髮

40. 答案：(C)

破 題 Does/Ms. Wallace/have/time...? ⇨ 問 Ms. Wallace「有沒有」時間。

解 析 (A) 時間字 ten thirty 為聯想錯誤，聽到問題中有 time，容易誤選。(B) 答非所問，這應該是和 Ms. Wallace 見面時所說的話。(C) 的 She can see you at three 回應了問題重點，為正確答案。

錄音內容 Does Ms. Wallace have any time on Thursday to meet with me?
(A) It's ten thirty now.
(B) It's nice to see you again.
(C) She can see you at three.

錄音翻譯 瓦歷斯小姐星期四有時間可以跟我見面嗎？
(A) 現在是十點半。
(B) 再次看到你很高興。
(C) 她三點可以見你。

Part ③

41. 答案：(B)

> **破題** What/man/say/presentation ⇨ 聽取男生說「簡報」的重點。
> **解析** 男子第一次發言中提到的 ... turn our presentation... into... 有題目關鍵字 presentation，而 turn... into 此片語的重點在 into 後面的 marketing presentation。故正確答案為包含 marketing 的 (B)。

42. 答案：(B)

> **破題** What/learned/presentation ⇨ 聽取關於「簡報」的特點或訊息。
> **解析** 本題未指明男女，由男子第二次發言中的 ... our presentation has... 即表示與 presentation 相關的訊息要出現了，由後面的 information about the materials we use。可確定答案為 (B)，而答案中 contains 對應了題目的 has，而 materials we use 則對應了 the company's products。

43. 答案：(D)

> **破題** What/company/sell ⇨ 聽取「產品名稱」，一定是「名詞」字眼。
> **解析** 由男子第二次發言中的 ... they're trying to promote our company as a leader in alternative flooring materials. 可知，正確答案為 (D)。

（錄音內容）

Questions 41 through 43 refer to the following conversation.

M: Kim wants us to turn our presentation on alternative flooring materials into a marketing presentation.

W: She wants that presentation to be for marketing? I'm surprised. It's just a small educational piece.

M: The fact that it IS an educational piece is why it makes sense. I mean, they're trying to promote our company as a leader in alternative flooring materials. Our presentation has a lot of information about the materials we use.

W: Yes, I guess you're right. I've never thought about it in terms of marketing material. Actually, it sounds like a fun project.

錄音翻譯

題目 41~43 請參照以下對話。

男：金要我們把替代地板材料的報告改成行銷報告。

女：她想把那篇報告做為行銷用嗎？我很意外。那只是一小篇教育用素材。

男：它是教育用素材這點就是它有意義的地方。我是說，他們打算把我們公司宣傳成替代地板材料的領導者。我們的報告裡有很多資料談到我們所使用的材料。

女：是，我想你說得對。我從來沒有從行銷內容的角度想過這點。事實上，它聽起來像是個有趣的案子。

題目&選項翻譯

41. 男子針對這份報告說了什麼？
    (A) 它差不多要完成了。
    (B) 它可以用於行銷。
    (C) 它應該要闡述得更完整。
    (D) 它比老闆所要的還長。

42. 關於這份報告我們可以知道什麼？
    (A) 它提供了公司的簡史。
    (B) 它包含了公司產品的相關資料。
    (C) 它顯示了銷售量在過去五年來有所增加。
    (D) 它描述了公司所提供的各種服務計畫。

43. 說話者的公司在販售什麼？
    (A) 影印機
    (B) 紙類產品
    (C) 辦公家具
    (D) 地板材料

- alternative [ɔlˋtɜnətɪv] *adj.* 替代的；二擇一的
- flooring material 地板材料
- make sense 有意義
- promote [prəˋmot] *v.* 宣傳；促進
- in terms of 就……而論
- actually [ˋæktʃuəlɪ] *adv.* 事實上
- fully [ˋfulɪ] *adv.* 完全地
- describe [dɪˋskraɪb] *v.* 描述
- copy machine 影印機

Questions 44~46

男：英 女：加

44. 答案：(D)

破 題 Why/woman/look for/new cell phone provider ⇨ 聽取女子要找新手機服務供應商的「原因」。

解 析 女子第一次發言提到 … looking into <u>different</u> options，different 表示會有改變，通常會有出題重點，而下一句的 I <u>haven't</u> been totally <u>satisfied</u>… <u>current</u> service provider 即為要改變的原因，故本題應選 (D)。注意，其中否定字眼 haven't 亦為聽力重點之一。

45. 答案：(A)

破 題 How long/man/new cell phone/service provider ⇨ 聽取男子說關於 cell phone 的「時間長度」。

解 析 男子第一次的發言提到 I <u>switched</u> to Cellular United about <u>a month ago</u>.，即表示使用「新的」provider service 有一個月了，故本題應選 (A)。

46. 答案：(C)

破 題 What/woman/want/know/man's cell ⇨ 聽取女子問與男子 cell phone 相關的資訊。

解 析 由女子第二次發言中的 Is the customer service good? 可知，答案為 (C)。

（錄音內容）

Questions 44 through 46 refer to the following conversation.

W: The contract for my cell phone plan is almost up, and I'm looking into different options. I haven't been totally satisfied with my current service provider. The signal is weak and a lot of my calls get cut off. Which company do you use?

M: I switched to Cellular United about a month ago.

W: And how are they? Is the customer service good?

M: So far, they're great. The signal is much better than it was with my last plan. In the month I've been with them, I haven't had to call customer service for anything, but they won some customer service award last year, so I assume they're good.

錄音翻譯

題目 44~46 請參照以下對話。

女：我的行動電話方案合約快要到期了，我正在研究不同的選擇。我對目前的服務業者並不是很滿意。他們的訊號微弱，而且我有很多通電話都被切斷。你用的是哪家公司？

男：我大概在一個月前換成了 Cellular United。

女：他們怎麼樣？客服好嗎？

男：到目前為止挺好的。他們的訊號比我上一個方案好多了。在我使用的這個月中，我還沒有什麼事需要打電話給客服，但是他們去年獲得某個客服獎項，所以我認為他們還不錯。

題目&選項翻譯

44. 女子為什麼在找新的行動電話服務業者？
   (A) 她打的電話很多。
   (B) 她需要一個不同的長途電話方案。
   (C) 她需要可以在歐洲使用的行動電話方案。
   (D) 她不滿意現有服務業者的客服。

45. 男子採用新的行動電話服務業者多久了？
   (A) 一個月
   (B) 四個月
   (C) 六個月
   (D) 一年

46. 對於男子的行動電話業者，女子想要知道什麼？
   (A) 他的方案要多少錢
   (B) 合約是多久
   (C) 客服怎麼樣
   (D) 他們有哪些手機

☐ contract [ˋkɑntrækt] *n.* 合約
☐ look into 深入地調查
☐ option [ˋɑpʃən] *n.* 選擇
☐ service provider 服務業者
☐ signal [ˋsɪgn!] *n.* 訊號

☐ cut off 切斷
☐ switch to 轉換到……
☐ long-distance [ˋlɔŋˋdɪstəns] *adj.* 長途的
☐ available [əˋveləb!] *adj.* 可買到的

MP3 108 **Questions 47~49**　　　　　　　　　　男：美　女：加

47. 答案：(B)

破題　committee's purpose ⇨ 聽取「目的」，即「主旨」。通常出現在對話第一句。

解析　女子第一次發言提到 I'm putting together a committee to look at efficiency in our department.，其中的不定詞 to look at 即表目的，而後面就是「主旨」。故本題選 (B)。

48. 答案：(A)

破題　When/Jack/return/office ⇨ 聽取 Jack 回 office 的「時間點」。

解析　由男子第一次發言中的 He should be back in the office around ten 可知，正確答案為 (A)。其實，男子在第二次發言又再度提到 Jack'll be back at ten，讀者有第二次的機會確定此題答案，但在考場上必須在第一次聽到時就立刻作答，以防沒有第二次機會。

49. 答案：(B)

破題　Why/woman/want/Jack/committee ⇨ 聽女子說「原因、理由」，通常為「好處」或「正面性」字眼。

解析　由女子第二次發言的 It would be nice to have some new voices on that committee. 以及第一次發言時問的 Do you think Jack would be willing to join? 即可推斷，正確答案為 (B)。注意，這裡以 bring a fresh perspective 代替 new voices。

錄音內容

Questions 47 through 49 refer to the following conversation.

W: I'm putting together a committee to look at efficiency in our department. Do you think Jack would be willing to join?

M: Um, I don't know him well enough to be able to answer that. But he seems pretty eager to get involved where he can. He should be back in the office around ten. You can talk to him then.

W: It would be nice to have some new voices on that committee. It's hard to know where you're losing efficiency when you're so involved. So far, everyone on the committee has been here for at least two years.

M: Yes, it would be good to have a new perspective. Jack'll be back at ten; you should talk to him about it.

Test 1

Part 1
Part 2
Part 3
Part 4
Test 2
Part 1
Part 2
Part 3
Part 4

簡
答

録音翻譯

題目 47~49 請參照以下對話。

女：我要組個委員會來檢視我們部門的效率。你想傑克會願意加入嗎？

男：嗯，我不是很了解他，所以沒辦法回答這點。不過他似乎很渴望能參與他可以發揮的事務。他應該會在十點左右回到辦公室，到時候你可以跟他談談。

女：如果那個委員有一些不同的聲音會很好。當你涉入很深時，就很難知道哪裡效率不彰。到目前為止，委員會裡的每個人起碼都到這裡兩年了。

男：對，有新的觀點是件好事。傑克十點會回來，你應該跟他談談這件事。

題目＆選項翻譯

47. 委員會的目的是什麼？

(A) 檢討方針

(B) 評估部門的效率

(C) 評估新產品

(D) 處理員工關切的事

48. 傑克什麼時候會回到辦公室？

(A) 早上十點

(B) 中午

(C) 下午一點

(D) 下午兩點

49. 女子為什麼希望傑克加入委員會？

(A) 他是地區經理。

(B) 他可以帶來新觀點。

(C) 他可以十分輕易地解釋複雜的事情。

(D) 他在公司裡擔任過很多職位。

□ put together 組合

□ committee [kə`mɪtɪ] *n.* 委員會

□ efficiency [ɪ`fɪʃənsɪ] *n.* 效率

□ be eager to + V 渴望做……

□ get involved (in) 涉入

□ perspective [pə`spɛktɪv] *n.* 觀點

□ purpose [`pɝpəs] *n.* 目的

□ policy [`paləsɪ] *n.* 政策

□ evaluate [ɪ`væljuɛt] *v.* 評估

□ address [ə`drɛs] *v.*（向……）提出；致力於

□ regional [`ridʒənl] *adj.* 地區的

□ complex [`kamplɛks] *adj.* 複雜的

□ position [pə`zɪʃən] *n.* 職位

Questions 50~52

男：英　女：澳

50. 答案：(C)

破題 Why/man/surprised ⇨ 聽取男子說「否定、負面」或「特殊」的字眼。

解析 男子第二次發言時說 I'm surprised he hasn't been by to pick them up yet.，通常 surprised 後面接的就是原因，故選 (C)。此處的 them 即指 samples。

51. 答案：(C)

破題 What/Seven/tell/man/he/do ⇨ 聽取與 Steven 相關的「動作」字眼。

解析 由男子第二次發言說的 He said he wanted to... go through the samples this morning and <u>place an order</u> this <u>afternoon</u>. 可知，本題應選 (C)。

52. 答案：(A)

破題 What/woman/offer/do ⇨ 聽取女子即將要做的「動作」字眼。

解析 女子說 If you want, I can <u>call him</u> and find out what's going on.，此處的 him 指的就是上一句中的 Steve，故本題應選 (A)。

[錄音內容]

Questions 50 through 52 refer to the following conversation.

M: Has Steve from Realto Fabrics come to pick up the box of samples yet?

W: No, his samples are still sitting here.

M: That's odd... Steve was insistent that we have the samples ready by this morning. He said he wanted to go through the samples this morning and place an order this afternoon. I'm surprised he hasn't been by to pick them up yet.

W: If you want, I can call him and find out what's going on.

Part 1
Part 2
Part 3
Part 4
Test 2
Part 1
Part 2
Part 3
Part 4
簡
答

录音翻譯

題目 50~52 請參照以下對話。

男：Realto Fabrics 的史帝夫來拿那箱樣品了沒？

女：沒有，他的樣品還放在這裡。

男：那就怪了……史帝夫堅持要我們在今天早上以前把樣品準備好。他說他想在今天早上檢視樣品，然後在今天下午下訂單。我很意外他還沒有來拿。

女：假如你要的話，我可以打電話給他，看看是怎麼回事。

題目&選項翻譯

50. 男子為什麼覺得意外？
    (A) 史帝夫還沒有付帳。
    (B) 史帝夫今天早上沒有出席會議。
    (C) 史帝夫沒有來拿一箱樣品。
    (D) 史帝夫沒有給理由就離開了辦公室。

51. 史帝夫告訴男子說他要做什麼？
    (A) 寄款項
    (B) 幫他完成一個案子
    (C) 在那天下午下訂單
    (D) 在開會時做簡報

52. 女子願意做什麼？
    (A) 打電話給史帝夫
    (B) 訂新的樣品
    (C) 幫忙男子做他的工作
    (D) 寄提醒付款通知

□ odd [ɑd] *adj.* 古怪的　　　　　□ pay the bill 付款

□ insistent [ɪnˋsɪstənt] *adj.* 堅持的　□ make a presentation 做簡報

□ go through 檢視　　　　　　　□ reminder [rɪˋmaɪdə] *n.* 催繳單

□ place an order 下訂單　　　　　□ notice [ˋnotɪs] *n.* 通知

MP3 110 **Questions 53~55**　　　　男：英　女：澳

53. 答案：(B)

破題 Why/man/call ⇨ 聽取男子打電話的「原因」。原因常為「主旨」，多出現在對話第一句。

解析 男子第一次發言說 Hello, Mary, this is Jeff. I'm running late so I'll...，通常 so 之前為「原因」，後為「結果」，故本題選 (B)。

54. 答案：(C)

破題 How many copies/man/has ⇨ 聽取男子說的「數量」字眼。

解析 由男子第二次發言說的 Yes, I have thirty copies of... 可知，本題應選 (C)。

55. 答案：(D)

破題 Where/speakers/plan/meet ⇨ 聽取兩人見面「地點」。

解析 由男子第一次發言時說的 ... I'll just meet you in Anderson's office... 及女子回應說的 Okay 可知，本題應選 (D)。

〔錄音內容〕

Questions 53 through 55 refer to the following conversation.

M: Hello, Mary, this is Jeff. I'm running late so I'll just meet you at the Anderson's office building.

W: Okay, but just go straight to his office—Anderson's office is number four twenty. Do you have copies of the report with you?

M: Yes, I have thirty copies of the report and I called to double-check that there's a projector set up for us. Everything is ready, but I'll be about five minutes late.

W: Thirty copies should be more than enough. I'll meet you in Anderson's office. I won't start until you arrive. Please hurry!

Part 1

Part 2

Part 3

Part 4

Test 2

Part 1

Part 2

Part 3

Part 4

錄音翻譯

題目 53~55 請參照以下對話。

男：哈囉，瑪莉，我是傑夫。我時間來不及，所以就和妳在安德森的辦公大樓會面了。

女：好，那就直接去他的辦公室——安德森的辦公室是四百二十號。你有沒有帶幾份報告在身上？

男：有，我帶了三十份報告，而且我打了電話去再次確認，他們有幫我們架設投影機。一切都準備好了，可是我大概會晚五分鐘。

女：三十份應該綽綽有餘。我會跟你在安德森的辦公室會面，等你到了再開始。請麻煩快點！

題目&選項翻譯

53. 男子為什麼打電話？
    (A) 他忘了一個檔案。
    (B) 他時間來不及。
    (C) 他需要投影機。
    (D) 他帶錯了磁碟。

54. 男子說他有有幾份報告？
    (A) 十份
    (B) 二十份
    (C) 三十份
    (D) 四十份

55. 說話者打算在哪裡會面？
    (A) 咖啡店
    (B) 火車店
    (C) 會議室內
    (D) 客戶的辦公室

- [ ] office building 辦公大樓
- [ ] double-check [ˋdʌblˋtʃɛk] v. 仔細檢查
- [ ] projector [prəˋdʒɛktə] n. 投影機
- [ ] set up 架設
- [ ] train station 火車站
- [ ] conference room 會議室

Questions 56~58

男：英 女：澳

56. 答案：(A)

破 題 What/man/think/company/do ⇨ 聽取男生說與公司有關的「動作」字眼。

解 析 由男子第一次發言的 We really need to think about <u>moving</u> to a <u>larger</u> space and <u>hiring</u> <u>more</u> financial <u>planners</u>. 可知，本題應選 (A)。注意，此處的 we 即 the company。

57. 答案：(B)

破 題 What/claim/man/make ⇨ 聽取男生提出的「論點」。

解 析 由男子第二次發言時說的 I think it <u>definitely</u> is. We have a <u>growing</u> client base—we have <u>twenty-five present</u> more client than we did a year ago. 可知，本題應選 (B)。注意，通常在 definitely 這類「強烈字眼」後會有出題重點，而特殊數字（如 25%）也是出題重點所在。

58. 答案：(C)

破 題 problem/woman/see/man's plan ⇨ 聽取女子說關於男子計畫的「否定或負面」字眼。

解 析 由女子的第二次發言的 ... <u>but</u> moving to a new office space <u>means</u> <u>shutting</u> <u>down</u> temporarily，可知應選 (C)。注意，通常 but 或 means 後面常有出題的線索。

錄音內容

Questions 56 through 58 refer to the following conversation.

M: We really need to think about moving to a larger space and hiring more financial planners.

W: I'm still not convinced that we do. Is it really worth the hassle and expense?

M: I think it definitely is. We have a growing client base—we have twenty-five percent more clients than we did a year ago. But we're at full capacity with the staff we have—we can't really take on any new business unless we hire more planners, and if we do that, we definitely need a larger office space.

W: Well, maybe you're right, but moving to a new office space means shutting down temporarily. And hiring new people... who's going to interview them? Who's going to train them after they're hired?

録音翻譯

題目 56~58 請參照以下對話。

男：我們真的需要考慮搬到更大的地方，並雇用更多的財務規劃人員。

女：我還是不認為有必要。真的值得大費周章花這些錢嗎？

男：我認為絕對值得。我們的客源愈來愈多——我們的客戶比一年前多了兩成五。可是我們已經把所擁有的人力運用到了極限，事實上我們沒有辦法再接任何新的生意，除非我們能雇用更多的規劃人員。而且假如我們這麼做，我們絕對需要更大的辦公空間。

女：好吧，也許你是對的，可是搬到新的辦公地點表示要暫時停工。還要雇用新人……誰要來面試他們呢？雇用之後，又要由誰來訓練？

題目&選項翻譯

56. 男子認為公司應該怎麼做？
   (A) 雇用額外的人員
   (B) 成立海外辦事處
   (C) 修訂財務策略
   (D) 打廣告來吸引新客戶

57. 男子提出的論點是什麼？
   (A) 過去打廣告吸引了很多的客戶。
   (B) 客戶的數目比一年前多了兩成五。
   (C) 找具備必要技術的工作人員並不難。
   (D) 現有辦公地點的租金超過該地區的平均水準。

58. 女子認為男子的計畫有什麼問題？
   (A) 必須編列新預算。
   (B) 他們無法及時籌到足夠的經費。
   (C) 辦公室將必須暫時關閉。
   (D) 有些工作人員必須重新分配到新部門去。

- ☐ financial [fə`nænʃəl] planner 財務規劃人員
- ☐ convinced [kən`vɪnst] *adj.* 確信的
- ☐ hassle [`hæsl] *n.* 【美】麻煩
- ☐ expense [ɪk`spɛns] *n.* 費用
- ☐ definitely [`dɛfənɪtlɪ] *adv.* 明確的
- ☐ at full capacity [kə`pæsətɪ] 運用到極限
- ☐ take on 承擔
- ☐ shut down 停業
- ☐ temporarily [`tɛmpə‚rɛrəlɪ] *adv.* 暫時地
- ☐ additional [ə`dɪʃənl] *adj.* 額外的
- ☐ overseas office 海外辦事處

- ☐ revise [rɪ`vaɪs] *v.* 修訂
- ☐ strategy [`strætədʒɪ] *n.* 策略
- ☐ advertise [`ædvə‚taɪz] *v.* （做）廣告
- ☐ attract [ə`trækt] *v.* 吸引
- ☐ make a claim 提出論點
- ☐ rent [rɛnt] *n.* 租金
- ☐ average [`ævərɪdʒ] *n.* 平均；平均數
- ☐ budget [`bʌdʒɪt] *n.* 預算
- ☐ raise money 籌款
- ☐ in time 及時
- ☐ reassign [‚riə`saɪn] *v.* 再分配

Questions 59~61　　　　男：英　女：加

59. 答案：(B)

破題　What/learned/speakers ⇨ 聽取兩人共同的「特殊或互動關係」字眼。

解析　由男子第二次發言時說的 I'd like to keep that channel that <u>shows</u> old movies. 及女子第二次發言時說的 I like those old movies too. 可知，本題應選 (B)。

60. 答案：(D)

破題　Why/speakers/want/reduce/cable service ⇨ 聽取「原因」字眼。因問題中有 reduce，所以應注意聽「否定、負面」意涵的關鍵字。

解析　由男子第一次發言時說的 Do you think we should <u>reduce</u>... <u>cable service</u>? 及 ... a <u>lot</u> of <u>channels</u>... <u>never</u>... look at and it seems <u>foolish</u> to <u>pay for</u> those. 可知，本題應選 (D)。

61. 答案：(B)

破題　What/woman/ suggest/man/do ⇨ 聽取女子表「建議」的字眼。

解析　女子第二次發言時說 <u>Why don't you</u> <u>call</u> the <u>cable</u> company to see... offer...?，其中的 Why don't you... 句型常用來表建議，因此本題應選 (B)。

錄音內容

Questions 59 through 61 refer to the following conversation.

M: Do you think we should reduce our cable service? Right now we have a lot of channels that we never even look at and it seems foolish to pay for those.

W: I think that's a good idea. We don't really watch that much television.

M: I'd like to keep that channel that shows old movies. I like that one. It's nice to turn on the TV and have a movie on, instead of sitcoms or sports.

W: I like those old movies too. Why don't you call the cable company to see what they can offer us?

(錄音翻譯)

題目 59~61 請參照以下對話。

男：妳認不認為我們應該減少有線電視的服務？目前我們有很多頻道是我們從來看都不看的，花錢在那些頻道上似乎很蠢。

女：我認為那是個好主意。我們其實並沒有看那麼多電視。

男：我想保留那個播老電影的頻道。我喜歡那台。它的好處是，打開電視就在播電影，而不是播情境喜劇或運動。

女：我也喜歡那些老電影。你何不打電話給有線電視公司，看看他們可以提供我們什麼？

(題目&選項翻譯)

59. 關於說話者我們可以知道什麼？
   (A) 他們是運動迷。
   (B) 他們都喜歡老電影。
   (C) 他們喜歡上電影院。
   (D) 他們看很多電視。

60. 說話者為什麼想減少有線電視的服務？
   (A) 最近費用漲了。
   (B) 免費試用期過了。
   (C) 他們想要節省開銷。
   (D) 他們擁有的頻道超過了他們的需要。

61. 女子建議男子做什麼？
   (A) 跟同事談談
   (B) 打電話給有線電視公司
   (C) 回應一項促銷優惠
   (D) 換一家新的有線電視服務業者

□ reduce [rɪ`djus] *v.* 減少

□ turn on 打開

□ sitcom [`sɪt.kɑm] *abbr.* 情境喜劇
   (= situation comedy)

□ fee [fi] *n.* 費用

□ recently [`risn̩tlɪ] *adv.* 最近

□ free trial period 試用期

□ cut one's expenses 節省開銷

□ coworker [`ko.wɜkə] *n.* 同事

□ respond to sth. 回應某事

MP3 113 **Questions 62~64**　　　　　　男：美　女：澳

62. 答案：(D)

破題 What/surprised/woman ⇨ 聽取女子表「驚訝」或「不解」的字眼。

解析 女子第一次發言中說的 I <u>didn't realize renting one</u> was a <u>possibility</u>! 是一個驚嘆句，其中的 one 代表上一句所說的名詞 large coffee maker，故本題應選 (D)。

63. 答案：(C)

破題 How much/cost/coffee maker/deliver/set up ⇨ 聽取與 coffee maker、deliver 等字眼有關的「價錢」字眼。

解析 由女子第二次發言時說的 So, if you <u>deliver</u> it and <u>set it up</u>, it's <u>twenty-five dollars</u>...? 可知，本題應選 (C)。

64. 答案：(A)

破題 How long/woman/need/coffee maker ⇨ 聽取女子說關於 coffee maker 的「時間長度」。

解析 由對話最後一句 We'll just <u>need</u> it <u>until</u> four <u>that day</u>. 可知，本題應選 (A)。

錄音內容

Questions 62 through 64 refer to the following conversation.

M: If you're only going to use the large coffee maker for large events a few times a year, it might be cheaper to just rent one, rather than buy one.

W: I didn't realize renting one was a possibility! I'd prefer that. We actually only need it for a few hours.

M: You can rent the coffee maker for fifteen dollars a day. If you want us to deliver it to your office and set it up with coffee and cream, it's an extra ten dollars.

W: So, if you deliver it and set it up, it's twenty-five dollars for the day? Great. Could I get a coffee maker delivered and set up with coffee and cream next Friday at 8 AM? We'll just need it until four that day.

錄音翻譯

題目 62~64 請參照以下對話。

男：假如妳是要在大型活動中使用大型咖啡機，而且一年只用幾次，那直接租一台可能
會比較便宜，而不要用買的。

女：我不曉得還可以租一台！我比較喜歡這樣。我們其實只需要用幾小時。

男：妳可以用十五美元租咖啡機一天。假如妳要我們把它送到妳們辦公室，並且把咖啡
和奶精裝好，那就要多付十美元。

女：所以，假如你們把它送去並裝好，那天就是收二十五美元囉？很好。我可以請你們
在下星期五早上八點送一台咖啡機過去，並且把咖啡和奶精裝好嗎？我們只需要用
到當天下午四點為止。

題目 & 選項翻譯

62. 什麼事讓女子感到意外？

(A) 咖啡機這麼大

(B) 咖啡機有多貴

(C) 咖啡機可以泡出多少咖啡

(D) 咖啡機可以租用

63. 請人運送並裝好咖啡機要花多少錢？

(A) 十五美元

(B) 二十美元

(C) 二十五美元

(D) 三十美元

64. 女子需要用咖啡機多久？

(A) 一天

(B) 兩天

(C) 三天

(D) 五天

☐ rent [rɛnt] *v.* 租用

☐ rather than 而不是

☐ deliver [dɪ`lɪvɚ] *v.* 運送

☐ extra [`ɛkstrə] *adj.* 額外的

☐ available [ə`veləbl̩] *adj.* 可取得的

MP3 114

Questions 65~67

男：美　女：加

65. 答案：(D)

破題 What/learned/man ⇨ 聽取「女人」對「男人的情況」的描述。

解析 女子第一發言說的 Did <u>you</u> and Mark go over <u>your lecture</u>? ... <u>You</u> do so many of <u>these</u>...，其中 these 指的是 lectures（演講），故本題應選 (D)。這裡以 deliver a lot of presentations 來代替 lectures。

66. 答案：(D)

破題 Where/lecture/held ⇨ 聽取與 lecture 有關的「場所」字眼。

解析 男子第一次發言時說的 I think... presenting <u>at the American Engineers Society</u>. 可知，本題應選 (D)。

67. 答案：(A)

破題 What/man/will/talk about ⇨ 聽取男子將談論的事，以「名詞」為主。

解析 由對話最後一句 I'll talk about the business... and about our <u>decision-making processes</u>. 可知，故本題應選 (A)。

錄音內容

Questions 65 through 67 refer to the following conversation.

W: Did you and Mark go over your lecture? What is this one on? You do so many of these, I can't keep them straight.

M: This lecture is on how we make components and our research processes. We just finished putting our slides together. I think both of us feel pressure presenting at the American Engineers Society—there are always a lot of important people there. We rearranged a lot of things.

W: So, what are you going to talk about?

M: Well, I'm going to cover general information about the company. I'll talk about how the business is run and about our decision-making processes.

錄音翻譯

題目 65~67 請參照以下對話。

W：你和馬克有沒有把你們的演講再溫習一遍？這次談的是什麼？你們做了太多次，我都記不清了。

M：這次演講談的是我們如何製造零組件，以及我們的研究過程。我們才剛把投影片整理好。我想我們兩個都覺得在美國工程師協會演講很有壓力，因為總是有許多重要人士在場。我們重新安排了很多東西。

W：那你們要談些什麼？

M：哦，我會介紹公司的概括資料。我會談談業務是如何運作的，以及我們的決策過程。

題目&選項翻譯

65. 關於男子我們可以知道什麼？
 (A) 他經常旅行。
 (B) 他是一位教授。
 (C) 他的工作時間很長。
 (D) 他發表過許多演講。

66. 演講會在哪裡舉行？
 (A) 大學
 (B) 募款活動上
 (C) 企業家聚會
 (D) 工程師協會的會議上

67. 男子說他要談些什麼？
 (A) 公司如何做決策
 (B) 他公司產品的眾多用途
 (C) 公司的各部門如何攜手合作
 (D) 他公司給員工的機會

☐ go over　重溫
☐ component [kəm`ponət] *n.*（機器、設備等的）零件
☐ put together　組合
☐ rearrange [ˌriə`rendʒ] *v.* 重新安排
☐ deliver [dɪ`lɪvə] *v.* 發表

☐ decision-making [dɪ`sɪʒənˌmekɪŋ] *n.* 做決策
☐ fundraising [`fʌndˌrezɪŋ] *n.* 募款
☐ entrepreneur [ˌantrəprə`nɝ] *n.* 企業家
☐ collaborate [kə`læbəˌret] *v.* 合作

Questions 68~70

MP3 115

男：美　女：澳

68. 答案：(A)

破題 What/learned/woman ⇨ 原則上，須聽取男子或女子說女子的「特點」。

解析 由女子第一次發言時說的 You know, I've been <u>coming</u> to this <u>hotel</u> for five years... 可知，女子之前來過這家飯店，故應選 (A)。

69. 答案：(D)

破題 what/new/hotel ⇨ 聽取與旅館有關的「新的事物」。

解析 由男子第二次發言時說的 We recently put <u>new furniture</u> in all the rooms. 即可知，本題應選 (D)。

70. 答案：(C)

破題 woman/say/will do ⇨ 聽取女子自己講未來會做的「動作」字眼。

解析 由女子第二次發言時說的 I'm planning to <u>come back again</u>. 即可知，本題應選 (C)。

(錄音內容)

Questions 68 through 70 refer to the following conversation.

M: Thank you for staying with us, Ms. Johnson. Was everything to your liking?

W: Yes, everything was great. You know, I've been coming to this hotel for five years now and each time I come it's better than the last.

M: I'm happy to hear that. We're trying to improve our offerings all the time. We recently put new furniture in all the rooms.

W: I thought it looked different. Very nice. Well, I'm planning to come back again on my vacation next year.

錄音翻譯

題目 68~70 請參照以下對話。

男：謝謝您來我們這裡住宿，強森女士。一切都合您的意嗎？

女：是的，一切都很好。你知道，我到現在光顧這家飯店五年了，而我每次來的時候，它都比上次更好。

男：我很高興聽到這點。我們一直在努力改進我們的設備服務。我們最近在所有的客房裡都擺放了新家具。

女：我想它看起來是不一樣。非常好。嗯，我打算明年度假時再回來。

題目＆選項翻譯

68. 關於女子我們可以知道什麼？
    (A) 她以前住過這家飯店。
    (B) 她在這家飯店住了五個晚上。
    (C) 她到過這家飯店來參加會議。
    (D) 她用信用卡付了飯店客房的費用。

69. 談話中提到飯店裡什麼是新的？
    (A) 費用
    (B) 菜單
    (C) 地毯
    (D) 家具

70. 女子說她將會做什麼？
    (A) 在中午時退房
    (B) 在飯店多住一晚
    (C) 明年再來
    (D) 把飯店推薦給她的朋友

□ to one's liking　合某人的意
□ offering [ˈɔfərɪŋ] *n.* 提供
□ all the time　始終
□ furniture [ˈfɜnɪtʃə] *n.* 家具
□ conference [ˈkɑnfərəns] *n.* 會議

□ credit card　信用卡
□ rate [ret] *n.* 費用；價格
□ check out　結帳離開
□ recommend [ˌrɛkəˈmɛnd] *v.* 推薦

Part ④

Part 1
Part 2
Part 3
Part 4
Test 2
Part 1
Part 2
Part 3
Part 4
簡答

MP3
117
Questions 71~73
美

71. 答案：(A)

破題 man/say/archives room ⇨ 聽取男子說 archives room 的相關字句。

解析 由第一行 The <u>archives room</u> is <u>hard</u> to <u>find</u>. 即可知，本題應選 (A)。注意，這裡用 difficult 代替 hard。

72. 答案：(A)

破題 man/look for ⇨ 聽取男子說「要找的東西」，聽名詞。

解析 第二行中的 look for 後面緊接的「名詞」a green door，就是答案，故選 (A)。

73. 答案：(D)

破題 Where/two steps ⇨ 注意聽與 two steps 相關的地方。

解析 由第三、四行的 Once you're inside, you'll see a <u>narrow</u> <u>hallway</u> to your right. <u>Walk down</u> that <u>hall</u>, and you'll find <u>two steps</u>. 可知，應選 (D)。

（錄音內容）
Questions 71 through 73 refer to the following talk.

The archives room is hard to find. The easiest way to get there is to go around to the left side of the warehouse and look for a green door. It's the only green door on the side of the warehouse. Once you're inside, you'll see a narrow hallway to your right. Walk down that hall, and you'll go down two steps. Just after you go down the steps look on your left, you should see a door that says "archives." That's where you want to go in.

（錄音翻譯）
問題 71~73 請參照以下獨白。

檔案室很難找。去那裡最簡單的方法就是到倉庫的左邊，找一扇綠門。它是倉庫那側唯一的綠門。你一進到裡面時，會在右手邊看到一條狹窄的走道。延走道走下去，你會往下走兩個階梯。走下這兩個階梯之後，往左邊看，你應該就會看到一扇門，上面寫著「檔案室」。那就是你要進去的地方。

題目&選項翻譯

71. 針對檔案室，男子說了什麼？

　　(A) 它很難找。

　　(B) 它在一樓。

　　(C) 它比他預期的要小。

　　(D) 它需要通關密碼才能進去。

72. 男子說要找到什麼？

　　(A) 一扇綠門

　　(B) 停車場

　　(C) 辦公總部

　　(D) 運貨電梯

73. 兩個階梯在哪裡？

　　(A) 辦公室外面

　　(B) 檔案室裡面

　　(C) 倉庫前面

　　(D) 狹窄走道的盡頭

☐ archives [ˋɑrkaɪvz] n. 檔案（室）　　　☐ access code [ˋæksɛs ͵kod] 進入密碼

☐ warehouse [ˋwɛr͵haʊs] n. 倉庫　　　☐ parking lot 停車場

☐ hallway [ˋhɔl͵we] n.【美】走廊　　　☐ freight [fret] elevator 運貨電梯

☐ step [stɛp] n. 台階

Part
1

Part
2

Part
3

Part
4

Test 2

Part
1

Part
2

Part
3

Part
4

簡
答

MP3
118 **Questions 74~76**   澳

74. 答案：(D)

破 題 Where/woman/work ⇨ 聽取女人工作的「地點」，若無法直接聽到該場所名稱，則要聽與該場所有關的字眼，通常是二到三個「名詞」或「動詞」。

解 析 由 第 一 行 中 的 ... the right <u>photo</u> to <u>enlarge</u>. You want the <u>picture</u>... <u>enlarged</u>...? 可推知，其工作場所應為 (D)。

75. 答案：(B)

破 題 How much/order ⇨ 聽取表「價錢」的字眼。

解 析 由第四行的 Okay, that total will be <u>twenty dollars</u>. 可知，正確答案為 (B)。

76. 答案：(A)

破 題 woman/offer/do ⇨ 聽取「動作」字眼。

解 析 第六句 If you want, I <u>can</u> <u>mail</u> it to you. 中的 it 即指 order，故選 (A)。

(錄音內容)

Questions 74 through 76 refer to the following talk.

Now, let me make sure I've written down the right photo to enlarge. You want the picture of the entire staff in front of the building enlarged to eleven by fourteen, right? I'm sure it will be nice to have a picture of the whole staff hanging in the lobby. Okay, the total will be twenty dollars. It'll be ready for you to pick up tomorrow by two o'clock. Or, if you want, I can mail it to you. If I mail it, it should get there by Friday. It's up to you.

(錄音翻譯)

問題 **74~76** 請參照以下獨白。

現在，讓我確定一下我有寫對你要放大的照片是哪一張。你想要把全體員工在大樓前面的那張照片放大到十一乘十四，對嗎？把全體員工的照片掛在大廳裡肯定會很不錯。好，總共是二十美元。明天兩點，你就可以來取件了。或者，假如你要的話，我可以寄給你。假如我用寄的話，星期五前應該會到。看你怎麼決定。

題目&選項翻譯

74. 女子可能是在哪裡工作？

   (A) 花店

   (B) 雜貨店

   (C) 辦公用品店

   (D) 相片沖洗中心

75. 訂貨要多少錢？

   (A) 十三美元

   (B) 二十美元

   (C) 一百二十美元

   (D) 兩百三十美元

76. 女子提議為顧客做什麼？

   (A) 郵寄訂貨

   (B) 替訂貨打折

   (C) 把訂貨的帳單記在信用卡上

   (D) 當天下午把訂貨送去

☐ make sure 確定

☐ enlarge [ɪn`lɑrdʒ] *v.* 放大

☐ staff [stæf] *n.* （全體）職員

☐ It's up to you. 由你決定。

☐ apply [ə`plaɪ] *v.* 使適用

☐ bill [bɪl] *v.* 開立帳單

MP3 119 **Questions 77~79** 英

77. 答案：(B)

破 題 What/expected/later/afternoon ⇨ 聽取「下午稍晚」的天氣狀況。

解 析 由第一行 Today in Crafton we should see <u>clearing skies</u> in the <u>afternoon</u> ... 可推斷，(B) 為正確答案。注意，fewer cloud 即代表 clearing skies。

注意 遇到這類先提到「答案」，才講到題目重點字眼的考題，一定要「先下手為強」，聽與題目有關的字眼，即立刻先去點選答案。

78. 答案：(D)

破 題 What/expected/Crafton/following evening ⇨ 聽取「隔天傍晚」的天氣狀況字眼。

解 析 由第三、四行 <u>Tomorrow</u>... partly cloudy... <u>Thundershowers</u> will be developed in the <u>evening</u>. 可知，本題應選 (D)。

79. 答案：(C)

破 題 What/current temperature/Crafton ⇨ 聽取 Crafton 的溫度。

解 析 由第五行的 Currently in <u>Crafton</u>, it's <u>fifty-two</u>... 即可知，正確答案為 (C)。

錄音內容

Questions 77 through 79 refer to the following weather report.

Today in Crafton we should see clearing skies in the afternoon with highs in the upper fifties. Tonight will be mostly clear with areas of frost developing after midnight. Lows in the low thirties. Tomorrow will be partly cloudy with highs in the lower forties. Thundershowers will develop in the evening and should last through the night, with lows in the upper thirties. Currently in Crafton, it's fifty-two under partly cloudy skies. For up-to-the-minute weather, login to our website at w-w-w dot weather dot crafton dot-com.

録音翻譯

問題 77~79 參照以下天氣預報。

今天下午在克福頓,我們應該會見到晴空,高溫在五十五度到五十九度之間。今晚大致晴朗,各地區在午夜過後會結霜,低溫在三十度到三十五度之間。明天晴偶有雲,高溫在四十度到四十四度之間。傍晚會有雷陣雨,而且應該會持續到夜晚,低溫在三十五度到三十九度之間。目前在克福頓,氣溫是五十二度,天氣晴偶有雲。欲知最新的氣象,請登入我們的網站:www.weather.crafton.com.。

題目&選項翻譯

77. 當天下午稍晚預計會怎麼樣?

　　(A) 雨比較多

　　(B) 雲比較少

　　(C) 停止下雨

　　(D) 雲量增多

78. 克福頓在隔天傍晚預計會怎麼樣?

　　(A) 下雪

　　(B) 有強風

　　(C) 天空晴朗

　　(D) 雷陣雨

79. 目前克福頓的氣溫是多少?

　　(A) 三十五度

　　(B) 四十六度

　　(C) 五十二度

　　(D) 六十度

□ high [haɪ] *n.* 高溫(←→low [lo] *n.* 低溫)
□ frost [frɑst] *n.* 霜
□ partly [ˈpɑrtlɪ] *adv.* 部分地
□ thundershower [ˈθʌdɚˌʃauɚ] *n.* 雷陣雨
□ last [læst] *v.* 持續

□ up-to-the-minute [ˌʌptəðəˈmɪnɪt] *adj.* 直到此刻的
□ following [ˈfɑloɪŋ] *adj.* 接著的
□ temperature [ˈtɛmpərətʃɚ] *n.* 溫度

MP3
120 **Questions 80~82** 加

80. 答案：(A)

破題 What event/discussing ⇨ 聽取「主旨」，通常為前三句中提到的「名詞」。

解析 由第二、三行 ... after the <u>trade show</u>... it's good... to <u>talk about</u> how <u>it</u> went. 即可推斷，正確答案為 (A)。注意，此處的 it 指的就是 trade show。

81. 答案：(D)

破題 What/speakers/want/audience/do ⇨ 聽取說話者與聽眾互動的「動作」字眼。

解析 第四行 <u>I'd like</u> to take this time... to <u>talk about things</u> that went <u>well</u> and <u>discuss what</u> we can <u>improve</u> for <u>next year</u>. 可知，本題應選 (D)。

82. 答案：(B)

破題 What/inferred/event ⇨ 應根據聽到有關 event 的字句來推測，但可先掃描一、兩個答案選項，作為推測的根據。

解析 由第二行中的 busy... <u>after</u> the <u>trade show</u> 及第四行中的 ... while it's <u>fresh in our head</u>... 可推知，本題應選 (B)。

[錄音內容]

Questions 80 through 82 refer to the following talk.

I want to thank each of you for coming to this meeting. I know you're all very busy catching up after the trade show, but it's good to get together after a big event to talk about how it went. I think this year's trade show was an amazing success, thanks to all of you. I'd like to take this time, while it's fresh in our heads, to talk about the things that went well and discuss what we can improve for next year. I'd like each of you to take a minute to think about the past week at the trade show and make your own list of things that worked and didn't work. Also think about how we compared to the other vendors that were there.

[錄音翻譯]

問題 80~82 請參照以下獨白。

我要謝謝各位來參加今天的會議。我知道大家都忙著在商展結束之後趕進度,但是在大型活動後能聚在一起聊聊它辦得怎麼樣也不錯。我認為今年的商展極為成功,這都多虧了大家。我想趁這個機會,也就是大家還記憶猶新的時候,來談談進行順利的事,並討論明年我們可以做些什麼改進。我想請各位花一分鐘想想過去這個星期的商展,並把自己認為奏效和行不通的事都列出來。同時想想跟現場的其他廠商比起來,我們表現得怎麼樣。

[題目 & 選項翻譯]

80. 說話者主要在討論什麼活動?
(A) 商展
(B) 會議
(C) 募款活動
(D) 比賽

81. 說話者要她的聽眾做什麼?
(A) 列出要感謝的人的名單
(B) 做出一份有關公司的簡報
(C) 討論一個增加公司獲利的策略
(D) 將明年要改進的事列成清單

82. 關於該項活動我們可以做出什麼樣的推論?
(A) 它持續十天。
(B) 它最近剛結束。
(C) 它將在不同的城市舉行。
(D) 它預定在下星期舉行。

□ catch up 趕上
□ trade show 商展
□ get together 聚在一起
□ improve [ɪmˋpruv] v. 改善
□ work [wɝk] v. 奏效;行得通
□ compare [kəmˋpɛr] v. 比較

□ vendor [ˋvɛndɚ] n. 販賣者
□ fundraiser [ˋfʌndˏrezɚ] n. 募款活動
□ competition [ˏkɑmpəˋtɪʃən] n. 競賽
□ audience [ˋɔdɪəns] n. 聽眾
□ hold [hold] v. 舉辦
□ schedule [ˋskɛdʒʊl] v. 預定

Part 1
Part 2
Part 3
Part 4
Test 2
Part 1
Part 2
Part 3
Part 4
簡答

MP3 121 **Questions 83~85**   美

83. 答案：(D)

破題 Who/speaker/work for ⇨ 聽取「公司、部門單位或人」的名稱。

解析 由第一行 ... we're going to begin <u>offering</u> our <u>clients</u> a new way to <u>advertise</u>. 可推斷，本題應選 (D)。另外，第九行 <u>We'll</u> <u>bill</u> our <u>clients</u> based on... <u>ad</u>... but also on... the <u>ad</u> is aired. 則為確認本題答案的第二個線索。

84. 答案：(C)

破題 Why/speaker/mention/fast food company ⇨ 聽取「原因、理由」字眼。

解析 由第四、五行 It offers our clients opportunities... <u>For example</u>, a <u>fast</u> <u>food</u> <u>restaurant</u> may want to <u>advertise</u>... 可知，應選 (C)。注意，通常在「舉例」之後會有出題線索。

85. 答案：(D)

破題 What/speaker/claim/company/done ⇨ 聽取說話者公司已做的「動作」字眼。

解析 由第八行 We've <u>measured</u> the amount of car and pedestrian <u>traffic</u> <u>at</u> <u>each location</u>, and <u>determined</u> the <u>peak traffic times</u>. 可知，本題應選 (D)。

錄音內容

Questions 83 through 85 refer to the following talk.

Next week we're going to begin offering our clients a new way to advertise: We're launching hundreds of digital billboards around the city that clients can buy time on. The billboards will be at bus stops, on street corners, on top of buildings—basically, it will be hard to go anywhere and not see one. It offers our clients opportunities they don't have with ordinary billboards. For example, a fast food restaurant may want to advertise breakfast items in the morning, lunch items in the afternoon, and dinner items in the evening; well, now they can. We've measured the amount of car and pedestrian traffic at each location, and determined the peak traffic times. We'll bill our clients based on the length of the ad—how many seconds it is—but also on when the ad is aired. We think we're going to be able to help our clients reach their target markets in new and more effective ways.

録音翻譯

問題 83~85 參照以下獨白。

下星期我們要開始為客戶推出一種新的廣告方式：我們會在市內設立好幾百個可供客戶購買時段的數位看板。這些看板會出現在公車站、街角、樓頂，基本上不管走到哪裡，都很難不看到它。它可以為客戶帶來一般看板上所沒有的機會。比方說，速食餐廳可能想要在早上宣傳早餐項目、在中午宣傳午餐項目、在晚上宣傳晚餐項目；嗯，現在他們做得到了。我們測量了各個地點的汽車和行人流量，並確定了交通尖峰時間。我們向客戶收費的依據是廣告的長度，也就是看有多少秒長，但廣告的播放時段也是一個依據。我們認為，我們將能以嶄新而且更有效的方式幫助客戶打入他們的目標市場。

題目 & 選項翻譯

83. 說話者可能在哪裡工作？
    (A) 銀行
    (B) 唱片公司
    (C) 電視台
    (D) 廣告公司

84. 說話者為什麼提到速食公司？
    (A) 為了說明客戶做了什麼
    (B) 為了描述他的典型客戶是些什麼人
    (C) 為了舉例說明客戶可以做什麼
    (D) 為了建議客戶應該去哪裡吃午飯

85. 說話者宣稱他的公司做了什麼？
    (A) 開發了新的金融產品
    (B) 協助全城好幾百家企業
    (C) 簽下了很多後來成名的無名藝術家
    (D) 測量城內不同地點的交通

- ☐ advertise [`ædvɚˌtaɪz] *v.* 做廣告
- ☐ launch [lɔntʃ] *v.* 將……投入市場
- ☐ billboard [`bɪlˌbord] *n.* 廣告牌
- ☐ measure [`mɛʒɚ] *v.* 測量
- ☐ pedestrian [pə`dɛstrɪən] *n.* 行人
- ☐ location [lo`keʃən] *n.* 地點
- ☐ determine [dɪ`tɝmɪn] *v.* 決定
- ☐ peak traffic time 尖峰交通時間
- ☐ bill [bɪl] *v.* 給……開帳單
- ☐ (be) based on 根據……

- ☐ second [`sɛkənd] *n.* 秒
- ☐ air [ɛr] *v.* 【美】播送
- ☐ target market 目標市場
- ☐ effective [ɪ`fɛktɪv] *adj.* 有效的
- ☐ illustrate [`ɪləstret] *v.* 說明
- ☐ typical [`tɪpɪkl] *adj.* 典型的
- ☐ claim [klem] *v.* 聲稱
- ☐ financial [faɪ`nænʃəl] *adj.* 金融的
- ☐ sign [saɪn] *v.* 簽約雇用

Part 1
Part 2
Part 3
Part 4
Test 2
Part 1
Part 2
Part 3
Part 4
簡
答

Questions 86~88 加

86. 答案：(C)

[破 題] What claim/speaker/made/herself ⇨ 聽取說話者對自己的「評論」。

[解 析] 由第二行 I perform better in stressful situations... 可知，本題應選 (C)。注意，此處用 work well 代替原句的 perform well，用 under pressure 代替原句的 in stressful situation。

87. 答案：(B)

[破 題] What/speaker/say/air traffic controller/able/do ⇨ 聽取 air traffic controller 能夠做的「動作」字眼。

[解 析] 第三行 You have to be able to make decisions quickly... 中的 You 即指做為一個 air traffic controller，故本題應選 (B)。

88. 答案：(C)

[破 題] What/speaker/imply/herself ⇨ 根據說話者說自己的情況來做推論。

[解 析] 由第六行的 I'm always thinking about the speed..., its attitude, its direction, what kind of planes... it's a lot to keep track of. 可看出，本句為「密集性排列」名詞考題，而最後一句即是綜合以上重點之意，故本題應選 (C)。

[錄音內容]

Questions 86 through 88 refer to the following talk.

I knew on my first day as an air traffic controller that I would be successful here. I perform better in stressful situations, and this job can be pretty intense. You have to be able to make decisions quickly, knowing that if you do make a bad decision, you'll have to fix it quickly. Everybody makes bad decisions sometimes, but here you can't change your mind, instead you have to figure out what to do to make it right. I'm always thinking about the speed of each aircraft, its altitude, its direction, what kind of planes are in the area... it's a lot to keep track of.

Part 1
Part 2
Part 3
Part 4
Test 2
Part 1
Part 2
Part 3
Part 4
簡答

(錄音翻譯)

問題 86~88 參照以下獨白。

我第一天作空中交通管制員的時候就知道,我在這裡會如魚得水。我在有壓力的情況下表現得更好,而這份工作會使人相當緊張。你必須有辦法迅速作決定,同時知道如果你真的決策失當,就必須迅速修正。每個人有時候都會決策失當,但是在這裡,你不能改變心意,而必須想辦法把事情矯正過來。我總是在考慮每班飛機的速度、高度、方向、當地有哪幾種飛機⋯⋯要掌握的事有很多。

(題目 & 選項翻譯)

86. 說話者宣稱她自己如何?
(A) 她過去是位駕駛員。
(B) 她從來不犯錯。
(C) 她在壓力下表現得很好。
(D) 她在世界上最繁忙的機場工作。

87. 說話者說空中交通管制員必須有辦法做到什麼?
(A) 像機師一樣思考
(B) 迅速作決定
(C) 運用專業術語
(D) 一次坐好幾個小時

88. 說話暗示她自己怎麼樣?
(A) 她會很快退休。
(B) 她幫忙拯救過許多人命。
(C) 她可以同時考量很多事。
(D) 她在國內各個機場服務過。

☐ air traffic controller 空中交通管制員
☐ perform [pəˋfɔrm] v. 執行;實行
☐ stressful [ˋstrɛsfəl] adj. 壓力重的
☐ intense [ɪnˋtɛns] adj. 劇烈的;強烈的
☐ make a decision 做決策
☐ figure out 理解;想出
☐ aircraft [ˋɛr͵kræft] n. 航空器(如飛機、飛船等)
☐ altitude [ˋæltə͵tjud] n. 高度
☐ direction [dəˋrɛkʃən] n. 方向
☐ keep track of 掌握
☐ make a mistake 犯錯
☐ under pressure 在壓力之下
☐ technical [ˋtɛknɪkl] adj. 技術的
☐ at a time 一次
☐ retire [rɪˋtaɪr] v. 退休

 **Questions 89~91**　　　　　　　　　　　　英

89. 答案：(A)

破題 What/speaker/say/hotels/Seattle ➾ 聽取對 Seattle 旅館的「評價」字眼。

解析 第一行 Finding an <u>affordable</u> <u>hotel</u> room in Seattle has gotten <u>really difficult</u>. 中提到的 really difficult 即為評價字眼，原句說該地的旅館很難負擔得起，也就是很昂貴，故本題應選 (A)。

90. 答案：(C)

破題 Which hotel/speaker/prefers ➾ 聽取說話者比較喜歡的旅館。

解析 說話者在第三、四行先提到 But it <u>doesn't</u> <u>make sense</u> to say <u>farther</u> away...，接著又說 <u>I mean</u>, you want to be right there, <u>near</u> the <u>site</u> of the <u>conference</u>.，也就是說，說話者希望住離會議中心近一點的旅館，故本題應選 (C)。

91. 答案：(B)

破題 What/speaker/say/he/do/if/organizing/conference ➾ 聽取「假設情況」下的「動作」字眼。

解析 第六行 ... if I were organizing a conference 之後的 I'd find a smaller, cheaper city. 即為答案，故本題應選 (B)。

（錄音內容）

Questions 89 through 91 refer to the following talk.

I was in Seattle for the Paper Packaging Convention last month. Finding an affordable hotel room in Seattle has gotten really difficult. Near the convention center, you can't get anything under a hundred and fifty a night. But it doesn't make sense to stay farther away when you're at a conference. I mean, you want to be right there, near the site of the conference. Seattle is a beautiful city, but if I were organizing a conference I'd find a smaller, cheaper city. Such expensive lodging really does prohibit small businesses from attending.

Part 1

Part 2

Part 3

Part 4

Test 2

Part 1

Part 2

Part 3

Part 4

(錄音翻譯)

問題 89~91 請參照以下獨白。

我上個月到西雅圖出席了紙類包裝大會。要在西雅圖找到一間負擔得起的旅館如今變得相當困難。在會議中心附近，你找不到任何一晚低於一百五十元的旅館。可是當你在開會期間，住得比較遠又不合情理。我的意思是，你想就住在當地，靠近開會的地點。西雅圖是個美麗的城市，可是假如是我舉辦會議，我會找個比較小而且比較便宜的城市。這麼昂貴的住宿真的大大阻礙了小企業的參與。

(題目&選項翻譯)

89. 說話者說西雅圖的旅館怎麼樣？

(A) 太貴了。

(B) 經常被預訂一空。

(C) 通常有網路折扣。

(D) 可以平價到令人意外。

90. 說話者說他比較喜歡住什麼樣的旅館？

(A) 最靠近海灘的旅館

(B) 最接近機場的旅館

(C) 靠近會議中心的旅館

(D) 遠離觀光景點的旅館

91. 說話者說，假如是他舉辦會議的話，他會怎麼做？

(A) 在夏天舉辦

(B) 在小城市舉辦

(C) 限制參加人數

(D) 提早敲訂日期

☐ affordable [əˋfɔrdəbl] *adj.* 負擔得起的

☐ make sense 合情理

☐ organize [ˋɔgəˏnaɪz] *v.* 組織；舉辦

☐ lodging [ˋlɑdʒɪŋ] *n.* 住宿

☐ prohibit [prəˋhɪbɪt] *v.* 阻礙

☐ be booked up 預訂一空

☐ surprisingly [səˋpraɪzɪŋlɪ] *adv.* 出奇地

☐ tourist site 觀光景點

☐ limit [ˋlɪmɪt] *v.* 限制

☐ in advance 預先

簡

答

MP3 124 Questions 92~94

澳

92. 答案：(D)

破題 What/Amy/say/never received ⇨ 聽取「否定」字眼後的「名詞」字眼。

解析 由第一行 ... this is Amy Dillon, I never received the spreadsheets... 即可知，本題應選 (D)。

93. 答案：(C)

破題 Who/Amy/indicate/another resource/office ⇨ 除 Amy 外，聽取另一個人的「名字或職稱」。

解析 由第四行 Jim，our office manager... 即可知，正確答案為 (C)。

94. 答案：(A)

破題 What/Amy/plans/do/evening ⇨ 聽取 Amy 提到有關 evening 的「動作」字眼。

解析 由第四句 I was hoping to look them over before writing my summary report this evening. 可知，應選 (A)。注意，句中有 before 或 after 時，要特別注意先後順序。

録音内容

Questions 92 through 94 refer to the following voicemail message.

Hi Daniel, this is Amy Dillon. I never received the spreadsheets you said you e-mailed to me. Is it possible for you to send them again? I was hoping to look them over before writing my summary report this evening. I'll be out of the office for a couple of hours. Jim, our office manager, knows I've been waiting for the spreadsheets. So, if you have any questions you can call back and talk to him. I hope to get those soon. Thanks.

録音翻譯

問題 92~94 請參照以下語音訊息。

嗨,丹尼爾,我是艾咪·狄隆。我並未收到你說你寄給我的試算表。可不可以再寄一次給我?我希望今晚在寫總結報告前能夠仔細看看。我會離開辦公室幾個小時,我們的辦公室經理吉姆知道我一直在等試算表。所以,如果你有任何問題,可以回電問他。希望我可以盡快收到,謝謝。

題目&選項翻譯

92. 艾咪·狄隆說她並未收到過什麼?

　　(A) 一張收據
　　(B) 一張發票
　　(C) 一份客戶檔案
　　(D) 試算表

93. 艾咪·狄隆指出她辦公室裡的另一位人手是誰?

　　(A) 她老闆
　　(B) 她的合夥人
　　(C) 辦公室經理
　　(D) 業務代表

94. 艾咪·狄隆說她當晚打算做什麼?

　　(A) 寫報告
　　(B) 關閉帳戶
　　(C) 更新資料庫
　　(D) 趕電子郵件

□ spreadsheet [ˋsprɛdˏʃit] *n.*【電腦】試算表
□ look over 仔細檢查
□ summary [ˋsʌmərɪ] *n.* 總結
□ receipt [rɪˋsit] *n.* 收據

□ invoice [ˋɪnvɔɪs] *n.* 發票
□ indicate [ˋɪndəˏket] *v.* 指出
□ sales representative 業務代表
□ close an account 關閉帳戶
□ catch up on sth. 趕完某事

Questions 95~97   英

95. 答案：(A)

破 題 What/speaker/do/China ⇨ 聽取 speaker 在 China 的「動作字眼」。

解 析 由第三行 Mostly Mr. Zhang and I spent time looking at our factories there in great detail. 可知，本題應選 (A)。

96. 答案：(B)

破 題 How/speaker/describe/people/met ⇨ 聽取所指的人之「特質」字眼，通常為形容詞。

解 析 由第二行 The people were very friendly and hospitable. 即可知，本題應選 (B)。

97. 答案：(B)

破 題 What/speaker/learned/company ⇨ 聽取任何有關公司「資訊」的字眼。

解 析 第八行 I never realized how much volume we produced. 中的 never realized 即表示說話者 learned 的東西，故本題應選 (B)。

錄音內容

Questions 95 through 97 refer to the following talk.

I got back from my business trip last night. It was incredibly interesting. I'd never been to China before and really had no idea what to expect. The people were very friendly and hospitable. Mostly Mr. Zhang and I spent time looking at our factories there in great detail. First we looked at the buildings and the general infrastructure, then the equipment that's used, and finally at the products. It was good to meet the people at the factory—I work with them every day by phone and e-mail, but I'd never met them before. It was quite interesting to see how a Chinese factory is run. I never realized just how much volume we produced. I mean, we never see it in this office. All we see are the financial figures.

Test 1

Part

1

Part

2

Part

3

Part

4

Test 2

Part

1

Part

2

Part

3

Part

4

簡

答

録音翻譯

問題 95~97 參照以下獨白。

我昨天晚上出差回來。這一趟真的十分有趣。我以前從來沒去過中國,所以完全不曉得會碰到什麼事。那裡的人十分友善和好客。我和張先生主要是花了一些時間仔細巡視我們在那裡的工廠。首先我們參觀了建築物和一般的基礎建設,接著看了所使用的設備,最後則是看產品。能見到工廠裡的人真不錯——我每天都透過電話和電子郵件和他們共事,但是過去從來沒見過他們。看到中國的工廠是如何運作的相當有趣,我從來不知道我們生產的東西量有多大。我是說,我們在這個辦公室裡從來沒看過,我們看到的都只是財務數字。

題目&選項翻譯

95. 說話者在中國做了什麼?

    (A) 巡視公司的工廠
    (B) 訓練工廠人員如何使用設備
    (C) 會見中國區域辦事處的主管
    (D) 稽核公司在那裡的辦事處

96. 說話者如何形容他在行程中所遇到的人?

    (A) 有創意
    (B) 友善
    (C) 有活力
    (D) 勤奮

97. 說話者說他了解了公司的什麼事?

    (A) 它的中國工廠經營得最棒。
    (B) 它生產了大量的產品。
    (C) 它花了很多錢訓練人員。
    (D) 它最好的產品是在中國廠製造的。

☐ business trip 出差
☐ incredibly [ɪn`krɛdəblɪ] adv. 難以致信地
☐ hospitable [`hɑspɪtəbl] adj. 好客的
☐ in great detail 詳細地
☐ infrastructure [`ɪnfrə͵strʌktʃə] n. 基礎建設
☐ equipment [ɪ`kwɪpmənt] n. 設備
☐ run [rʌn] v. (機器等)運轉
☐ volume [`vɑljəm] n. (生產或交易等的)量

☐ figure [`fɪgə] n. 數據
☐ conduct [kən`dʌkt] v. 處理;經營
☐ audit [`ɔrdɪt] n. 稽核
☐ energetic [͵ɛnə`dʒɛtɪk] adj. 精力旺盛的
☐ hard-working [`hɑrd`wɜkɪŋ] adj. 勤奮的

_{MP3}
₁₂₆ **Questions 98~100** 加

98. 答案：(C)

破題 Who/speaker/addressing ⇨ 聽取與說話者說話「對象」有關的字句。

解析 由第六行 If you need help, ask..., they've both been here for three years and know all the tricks. 可推斷，本題答案為 (C)。另，第七、八行的 Of course, you can really ask anyone. People are eager to help around here.，亦表示聽者為 (C)。

99. 答案：(C)

破題 What/speaker/discuss ⇨ 聽取「主旨」，通常在前三句。

解析 由第一行 Okay, one last point... 可知，其後即為主要討論的內容。由 Now, you can schedule a meeting in the conference room through our intranet. 可知，本題應選 (C)。

100. 答案：(D)

破題 What/said about/Sue/Peter ⇨ 聽取有關 Sue 和 Peter 的字句。

解析 第六行 If you need help, ask Sue or Peter, they've both been here for three years and know all the tricks. 即可知，本題應選 (D)。注意，If 後面所接的內容，常為出題重點。

〔錄音內容〕

Questions 98 through 100 refer to the following talk.

Okay, one last point and we're done here. Now, you can schedule a meeting in the conference rooms through our intranet. It's easy to do. Once you log on, you'll see a link to room scheduling and from there you just follow the directions. You can also request supplies to be brought into the conference rooms. So if you need a projector or an extra laptop, the tech crew will set that stuff up for you. If you need help, ask Sue or Peter, they've both been here for three years and know all the tricks. Of course, you can really ask anyone. People are eager to help around here.

[錄音翻譯]

問題 98~100 請參照以下獨白。

好，剩最後一點我們就結束了。現在，你可以透過我們的內部網路預約會議室的開會時間。這很容易做。一旦你登錄後，你會看到預約會議室的連結，接下來只要遵照指令就可以了。你還可以要求在會議室裡備妥用品，所以假如你需要投影機或額外的筆記型電腦，科技組人員就會幫你把那些東西準備好。假如你需要幫忙，可以找蘇或彼得。他們兩個在這裡都已經待了三年，什麼竅門都知道。當然，其實你問什麼人都可以。在這裡大家都會熱心地幫忙。

[題目&選項翻譯]

98. 說話者可能是在對誰說話？
   (A) 客戶
   (B) 供應商
   (C) 新進員工
   (D) 飯店經理

99. 說話者主要在討論什麼？
   (A) 租投影機
   (B) 替訪客安排
   (C) 預約會議室
   (D) 籌備產品展示

100. 關於蘇和彼得說話者提到什麼？
   (A) 他們會帶設備來。
   (B) 他們會備妥會議室。
   (C) 他們應該受邀與會。
   (D) 假如有需要的話，他們可以幫忙。

☐ intranet [ˈɪntrəˌnɛt] *n.* 【電腦】內部網路
☐ log on 【電腦】登錄
☐ supply [səˈplaɪ] *n.* 供給
☐ laptop [ˈlæpˌtɑp] *n.* 膝上型電腦
☐ tech [tɛk] *n.* 科技 (= technology)
☐ crew [kru] *n.* 全體組員

☐ trick [trɪk] *n.* 竅門
☐ be eager to + V 熱切想做……
☐ supplier [səˈplaɪɚ] *n.* 供應商
☐ reserve [rɪˈzɝv] *v.* 預約
☐ demonstration [ˌdɛmənˈstreʃən] *n.* 展示

Test 2 完整解析

Part ①

1. 答案：(C)　美

> **圖　析** 公園裡有一名女子坐著看報紙，背對著一座有柵欄的花圃。

> **解　析** 本題考動詞。(A) recycling、(B) buying 及 (D) folding 等動詞皆與照片不符，只有 (C) 動詞 reading 及受詞 newspaper 與圖片一致，故為正確答案。

> **錄音內容** (A) She's recycling newspapers.
> (B) She's buying a newspaper.
> (C) She's reading a newspaper.
> (D) She's folding newspapers.

> **錄音翻譯** (A) 她在回收報紙。
> (B) 她在買報紙。
> (C) 她在看報紙。
> (D) 她在摺報紙。

> ☐ recycle [rɪˋsaɪkl] *v.* 回收　　　☐ fold [fold] *v.* 折疊

2. 答案：(C)　加

> **圖　析** 一名女子在公共電話亭內使用電話。

> **解　析** 本題主要考受詞。 (A) cell phone（手機）、(B) microphone（麥克風）和 (D) crowd（群眾）皆與照片不符，只有 (C) 動詞 using 及受詞 a public telephone 與圖片一致，故為正確答案。

> **錄音內容** (A) She's using a cell phone.
> (B) She's talking into a microphone.
> (C) She's using a public telephone.
> (D) She's speaking to a crowd.

> **錄音翻譯** (A) 她在用行動電話。
> (B) 她在對麥克風講話。
> (C) 她在用公共電話。
> (D) 她在對群眾說話。

> ☐ cell phone 行動電話　　　☐ public telephone 公共電話
> 　 (= cellular phone)　　　☐ crowd [kraʊd] *n.* 人群
> ☐ microphone [ˋmaɪkrəˏfon] *n.* 麥克風

Test 1

Part 1

Part 2

Part 3

Part 4

Test 2

Part 1

Part 2

Part 3

Part 4

簡

答

3. 答案：(D)　　　　　　　　　　　　　　　　　　　　　英

圖析 一名男子背對著鏡頭，坐在公園裡的岩石上。他的前面有一、兩棵樹。

解析 本題考動詞。(A) lifting（舉起）與 (B) throwing（丟）都不對，而 (C) listening to rock 指的是聽搖滾樂，也不對，故 (D) 為正確答案。

錄音內容 (A) He's lifting the rock.
　　　　　 (B) He's throwing a rock.
　　　　　 (C) He's listening to rock.
　　　　　 (D) He's sitting on a rock.

錄音翻譯 (A) 他正舉起石頭。
　　　　　 (B) 他在丟石頭。
　　　　　 (C) 他在聽搖滾樂。
　　　　　 (D) 他坐在石頭上。

☐ lift [lɪft] *v.* 舉起　　　　　　☐ rock [rɑk] *n.*【音】搖滾樂

4. 答案：(D)　　　　　　　　　　　　　　　　　　　　　美

圖析 打開的冰箱，裡面擺放著各種不同的食物。

解析 本題考動詞及受詞。(A) served 及 restaurant 皆錯；(B) cooking 及 stove 不對；(C) sold 及 supermarket 亦錯，故正確答案為 (D)。注意，本題中的「被動語態」使用，常為聽力的命題重點，平常要多練習主動、被動語態的轉換。

錄音內容 (A) The food is being served at a restaurant.
　　　　　 (B) The food is cooking on the stove.
　　　　　 (C) The food is being sold at a supermarket.
　　　　　 (D) The food is kept cold in a refrigerator.

錄音翻譯 (A) 餐廳裡正在供應食物。
　　　　　 (B) 爐子上正在烹煮著食物。
　　　　　 (C) 超市裡正在出售食物。
　　　　　 (D) 冰箱裡冷藏著食物。

☐ stove [stov] *n.* 火爐　　　　　☐ refrigerator [rɪˋfrɪdʒəˌretə] *n.* 冰箱

5. 答案：(A) 美

圖 析 一張文件正從傳真機中列印出來。

解 析 本題考動詞。(A) printed 與照片相符，為正確答案。(B) loaded（裝入）、(C) dropped（掉落）及 (D) shredded（切成碎片）皆與照片不符。

錄音內容 (A) A page is being printed.
(B) The paper is being loaded into the photocopier.
(C) A page has been dropped on the floor.
(D) The paper is being shredded.

錄音翻譯 (A) 有一頁正在列印。
(B) 紙正被裝入影印機裡。
(C) 有一頁掉到了地上。
(D) 紙正被切碎。

☐ load [lod] *v.* 裝入　　　　　　　　☐ drop [drɑp] *v.* 掉落
☐ photocopier [ˈfotəˌcɑpɪə] *n.* 影印機　☐ shred [ʃrɛd] *v.* 切成碎片

6. 答案：(A) 加

圖 析 一個手中握著脆餅的小孩，在公園內騎坐在父親的肩膀上。

解 析 本題需注意主詞是 child 還是 father，來對應正確的動詞。(A) 主詞 child、動詞 riding 及受詞 shoulders 皆正確，故為正確答案。(B) put his child in a stroller（嬰兒車）與照片不符；(C) 動詞 picking up 錯誤；(D) 也不對，因為 holding pretzel 的主詞應為 child。

錄音內容 (A) The child is riding on his father's shoulders.
(B) The father has put his child in a stroller.
(C) The child is picking up a pretzel.
(D) The father is holding the child's pretzel.

錄音翻譯 (A) 小孩正騎在爸爸的肩膀上。
(B) 爸爸把小孩放在嬰兒車裡。
(C) 小孩正在撿脆餅。
(D) 爸爸拿著小孩的脆餅。

☐ shoulder [ˈʃoldə] *n.* 肩膀　　　　☐ pick up 撿起
☐ stroller [ˈstrolə] *n.*【美】折疊式嬰兒車　☐ pretzel [ˈprɛtsl] *n.* 椒鹽脆餅

Test 1

Part
1

Part
2

Part
3

Part
4

Test 2

Part
1

Part
2

Part
3

Part
4

簡

答

7. 答案：(D)　　　　　　　　　　　　　　　　　　　　　　　　　英

圖 析 有一堆盒子被堆放在架子上。

解 析 (A) 動詞 sealed 不對；(B) 動詞 loaded 及介系詞片語中之 truck 皆錯；(C) 主詞 boxers（拳擊手）與動詞片語 warming up 皆錯。本題應選 (D)，動詞 stacked 及 shelves 皆與照片吻合。注意，本題亦需留心主被動的應用。

錄音內容 (A) The boxes are being sealed.
(B) The boxes have been loaded on a truck.
(C) The boxers are warming up.
(D) The boxes are stacked on the shelves.

錄音翻譯 (A) 箱子正在封裝。
(B) 箱子已經裝載上了貨車。
(C) 拳擊手正在熱身。
(D) 箱子堆在架子上。

□ seal [sil] *v.* 密封　　　　　　　□ stack [stæk] *v.* 疊堆
□ boxer [`bɑksɚ] *n.* 拳擊手　　　　□ shelf [ʃɛlf] *n.* 架子
□ warm up　暖身

8. 答案：(B)　　　　　　　　　　　　　　　　　　　　　　　　　澳

圖 析 一位男子在博物館內，看著一座雕像。

解 析 (A) 動詞 making 錯誤；(C) 也錯，因為無法從照片判斷是 taking an art calss（上美術課）；(D) gymnasium（健身房）地點錯誤。故本題應選 (B) The man in a museum。

錄音內容 (A) The man is making a statue.
(B) The man is in a museum.
(C) The man is taking an art class.
(D) The man is in a gymnasium.

錄音翻譯 (A) 這位男子在做雕塑。
(B) 這位男子在博物館裡。
(C) 這位男子在上美術課。
(D) 這位男子在健身房裡。

□ statue [`stætʃʊ] *n.* 雕像　　　　　□ gymnasium[dʒɪm`nezɪəm] *n.* 體育館；
□ take a class　上課　　　　　　　　健身房

9. 答案：(B)　　　　　　　　　　　　　　　　　　　　　　　美

圖析 一些人走在飛機場內的電動走道上。

解析 (A) 主詞 airplanes 不對；(C) 以動詞 moved 混淆圖片中的 moving walkway，為相似音陷阱；(D) 動詞 boarding 錯誤。(B) 主詞 people、動詞 uising 及受詞 moving walkway 皆無誤，故為正確答案。

錄音內容 (A) The airplane is landing at the airport.
(B) People are using a moving walkway.
(C) The airport is being moved to another location.
(D) People are boarding the aircraft.

錄音翻譯 (A) 飛機正降落在機場。
(B) 人們在用電動步道。
(C) 機場正被遷往另一個地方。
(D) 人們正在登機。

□ land [lænd] *v.* 降落
□ moving walkway 電動步道
　(= moving sidewalk)
□ location [loˋkeʃən] *n.* 地點
□ board [bord] *v.* 上（船、車、飛機等）
□ aircraft [ˋɛrˌkræft] *n.* 航空器（飛機、飛船等）

10. 答案：(B)　　　　　　　　　　　　　　　　　　　　　　　加

圖析 有一個人手上拿著現金，要放入皮夾內。

解析 (A) 的 cashing 為「換現金」，而圖中看到則是 cash（現金）。(C) 為「聯想」陷阱，看到錢就會想到 paying（付錢）。(D) taking notes 與照片不符。(B) 的關鍵字 putting、money、in his wallet 與圖片一致，為正確答案。

錄音內容 (A) He's cashing a check.
(B) He's putting money in his wallet.
(C) He's paying a bill online.
(D) He's taking notes.

錄音翻譯 (A) 他在兌現支票。
(B) 他正把錢放進皮夾裡。
(C) 他正在網上付帳。
(D) 他在做筆記。

□ cash a check 兌現支票
□ wallet [ˋwɑlɪt] *n.* 皮夾
□ bill [bɪl] *n.* 帳單
□ take notes 做筆記

Part ②

MP3 **139** ▶▶ MP3 **168**

Test 1

Part 1

Part 2

Part 3

Part 4

11. 答案：(C)

加 ▶ 英

破 題 Why did you...? ⇨ 問「原因」。

解 析 Why 開頭的問句，要以表「原因」的答案對應之。(A) 主詞不對，應該用 I 回答。注意，You did? 通常表「驚訝或不相信對方的話，在本題中文不對題。(B) Why 問句不可用 Yes 或 No 回答。故正確答案為 (C)，以 better offer 來解釋 turn down the job 的原因。

錄音內容 Why did you turn down the job at Fitzgerald's?
(A) You did? That surprises me.
(B) No, I decided not to take it.
(C) I got a better offer from DrayCo.

錄音翻譯 你為什麼拒絕費滋傑羅的工作？
(A) 你拒絕了嗎？那真令我驚訝。
(B) 不是，我決定不接受。
(C) 我從德瑞柯那裡獲得了更好的條件。

☐ turn down 拒絕　　　　☐ offer [ˋɔfɚ] *n.* 出價；報價；願提供的事物

12. 答案：(A)

美 ▶ 英

破 題 Dan has..., hasn't he? ⇨ 考「附加問句」，要以 Yes 或 No 來回答。

解 析 (A) 用 Yes 表同意前半句的敘述，而 it 則代表了 Dan 不在的時間，為正確答案。(B) 文不對題，題目問 Dan，但答案卻以 me 和 my 為回答重點。(C) 答非所問，附加問句不應以另外一個問句來回答，否則還是不知「是或不是」。

Part 2

錄音內容 Dan has been out for a couple of weeks, hasn't he?
(A) Yes, it's been a while now.
(B) Let me check my schedule.
(C) Really? Where are you going?

錄音翻譯 丹不在好幾個星期了，不是嗎？
(A) 是的，到現在已經有好一陣子了。
(B) 我來查查我的行程。
(C) 真的嗎？你要去哪？

☐ be out 外出　　　　☐ a while 一陣子

13. 答案：(A)

澳 ▶ 美

破 題 Have/you/considered/outsourcing...? ⇨ 問「有或沒有」考慮外包。

解 析 (A) 為正確答案，用 have to 表 Yes，回應了問題，而 have to 後面省略掉重點字 consider outsourcing。(B) 主詞也不對，且不應用問句回應。(C) 回答 No，表示不考慮，接著又提到 company in New York，前後矛盾。

錄音內容 Have you considered outsourcing part of the job?
　　　　(A) We may have to.
　　　　(B) Why did you do that?
　　　　(C) No, a company in New York.

錄音翻譯 你們有沒有想過把部分的工作外包？
　　　　(A) 我們可能非這樣做不可。
　　　　(B) 你們為什麼要這麼做？
　　　　(C) 沒有，是一家紐約的公司。

☐ consider [kən`sɪdə] v. 考慮　　　☐ outsourcing [͵aut`sɔrsɪŋ] n. 外包（工作）

14. 答案：(C)

加 ▶ 英

破 題 Who/should/I/talk to...? ⇨ 問「人名」、「職稱」或「部門單位」。

解 析 (A) 主詞 It 錯誤，且並未指出「誰」。(B) Wh 開頭的問句，不可以 Yes 或 No 回答。(C) Accounts payable（應付帳款部）表「單位」，故為正確答案。

錄音內容 Who should I talk to about overdue bills?
　　　　(A) It doesn't happen that often.
　　　　(B) No, not according to my records.
　　　　(C) Accounts payable, on the third floor.

錄音翻譯 關於逾期帳單，我該找誰談？
　　　　(A) 那沒有那麼常發生。
　　　　(B) 沒有，根據我的記錄並沒有。
　　　　(C) 應付帳款部，在三樓。

☐ overdue [ˋovəˋdju] adj. 逾期的　　　☐ record [ˋrɛkəd] n. 記錄
☐ bill [bɪl] n. 帳單　　　☐ accounts payable 應收帳款
☐ according to 根據

Test 1

Part
1

Part
2

Part
3

Part
4

Test 2

Part
1

Part
2

Part
3

Part
4

簡

答

15. 答案：(B)

澳▶美

破 題 Whose report/you/planning/read...? ⇨ 問要先讀「誰的」報告。

解 析 (A) 答非所問，both... good 與題目重點 read first 無關。(C) 文不對題，good 在此無法呼應問題重點。(B) 主詞 I 正確，而 yours 即代表 your report。注意，本題結合了「資訊性」及「選擇性」問題，但重心在後面的選擇。

錄音內容 Whose report are you planning to read first, mine or Liz's?
(A) They were both very good.
(B) I'm about to start on yours.
(C) Good, I'm looking forward to it.

錄音翻譯 你打算先看誰的報告，我的還是麗茲的？
(A) 它們都非常好。
(B) 我將從你的看起。
(C) 好，我很期待。

□ be about to do 即將做   □ look forward to + Ving 期待……

16. 答案：(A)

澳▶加

破 題 Do/you/have/allergies? ⇨ 問「有沒有」過敏。

解 析 (A) No 回答了題目重點，none 也呼應了「沒有」，為正確答案。(B) 答非所問，a lot of people 與問題無關。(C) 為「聯想陷阱」，聽到 allergies，就想到 doctor，但原句為問句，不應以問句回應。

錄音內容 Do you have any allergies?
(A) No, none that I'm aware of.
(B) Yes, I know, a lot of people have.
(C) Have you seen a doctor for that?

錄音翻譯 你有任何過敏嗎？
(A) 沒有，我知道的並沒有。
(B) 是的，我知道，有很多人有。
(C) 你有沒有就那點去看過醫生？

□ allergy [ˋælədʒɪ] n.【醫】過敏症   □ see a doctor 看診
□ be aware of 意識到

17. 答案：(A)

加 ▶ 澳

破 題 Were/able/find/everything/needed? ⇨ 問「是不是能夠」找到需要的東西。

解 析 (A) Yes 回應題目 Were 的問句，而 no problem 則呼應了問題中 able 和 find，故為正確答案。(B) 答非所問。(C) don't 及 I'll 時態有誤，原句用的是過去式 were 來問。

錄音內容 Were you able to find everything you needed?
(A) Yes, I had no problems, thank you.
(B) Please let me know if I can help you.
(C) I don't think I'll help with everything.

錄音翻譯 你是不是能夠找得到你所需要的一切？
(A) 是的，沒問題，謝謝。
(B) 假如我能幫你忙，請告訴我一聲。
(C) 我想我並不會幫忙處理一切。

18. 答案：(B)

加 ▶ 美

破 題 Isn't/there/another/bus...? ⇨ 以 Isn't 開頭的否定問句，要回答 Yes 或 No。

解 析 (A) 答非所問，Oh no 表「糟了」，此為「借字混淆」，不可聽到 no 以為是「不是」而選它。(C) didn't 為過去式與原句 Isn't 時態不符。故應選 (B)，There's supposed to be. 的意思是「應該有」。

錄音內容 Isn't there another bus at three?
(A) Oh no, do you know why?
(B) There's supposed to be.
(C) I didn't think so either.

錄音翻譯 三點沒有另一班公車嗎？
(A) 糟了，你知道為什麼嗎？
(B) 應該有。
(C) 我也不這麼認為。

□ be supposed to 應該

Test 1
Part 1
Part 2
Part 3
Part 4
Test 2
Part 1
Part 2
Part 3
Part 4
簡
答

19. 答案：(A)　　　英▶美

破題 introduction/seemed/long ⇨「直述句」，要了解說話者的重點意圖。

解析 (A) It 代表了 introduction, did 指 seemed... long，故為正確答案。(B) 直述句不用 Yes 或 No 回答，且 introduced 企圖混淆原句重點字 introduction。(C) 不知所云，未回應題目重點。

錄音內容 The introduction seemed a little long to me.
(A) It did to me as well.
(B) Yes, we've been introduced.
(C) Who's writing the introduction?

錄音翻譯 我覺得前言似乎長了點。
(A) 我也這麼覺得。
(B) 是的，我們被介紹過了。
(C) 誰在寫前言？

☐ introduction [ˌɪntrəˈdʌkʃən] *n.* 前言；引言

20. 答案：(A)　　　加▶美

破題 Have/traveled/tropical/countries ⇨ 問「有或沒有」到過熱帶國家。

解析 (A)的 Yes 回答了題目重點，Brazil 和 last year 則明確指出所去的地方和時間。(B) 用 Neither have I 表「我也沒有」，不符合問題。(C) 主詞 it 不對，因為問的是 you，而且內容答非所問。

錄音內容 Have you traveled to any tropical countries in the past three years?
(A) Yes, I was in Brazil last year.
(B) Neither have I, but I'd love to.
(C) Well, it sounds like you had fun.

錄音翻譯 過去三年裡，你有沒有去過任何熱帶國家？
(A) 有，我去年去了巴西。
(B) 我也沒有，但我很想。
(C) 嗯，聽起來你玩得很開心。

☐ tropical [ˈtrɑpɪkl] *adj.* 熱帶的　　☐ have fun 玩得開心
☐ sound like 聽起來

21. 答案：(B)

澳▶美 加▶美

破 題 When/you/send/payment? ⇨ When 為首的問句，要以「時間」來回答。

解 析 (A) 不知所云，amount（數量）非題目所問。(C) 答非所問，問句問的是「時間」而非「好不好」。(B) 的 last Friday 回答了重點，且動詞用過去式 sent，符合原句時態。

錄音內容 When did you send your payment?
(A) For the full amount.
(B) I sent it last Friday.
(C) Good, I'll look for it.

錄音翻譯 你是什麼時候寄出你的款項的？
(A) 全額。
(B) 我是上星期五寄的。
(C) 好，我來找找看。

□ payment [ˋpemənt] *n.* 付款   □ full amount 全額

22. 答案：(B)

澳▶美

破 題 VitalCom/going to give/us/competition/don't you think? ⇨ 直述句 + 附加問句，要回答「是或不是」。

解 析 (A) 的時態不對，原句為 is going to，表「將要」。(C) 答非所問，great 無法回應原句的 give us... serious competition。(B) 的 Yes 回答了題目重點，they 指 Vital Com，而 our main competition 則對應了題目中的 give us serious competition。

錄音內容 VitalCom is going to give us some serious competition for the project, don't you think?
(A) Did they, really? I'm surprised.
(B) Yes, they're usually our main competitors.
(C) The VitalCom project would be great for us.

錄音翻譯 VitalCom 在這個案子上會跟我們有一些激烈的競爭，你不覺得嗎？
(A) 他們真的有嗎？我很驚訝。
(B) 是啊，他們一向是我們的主要競爭者。
(C) VitalCom 的案子對我們非常好。

□ competition [ˌkampəˋtɪʃən] *n.* 競爭   □ competitor [kəmˋpɛtətə] *n.* 競爭者

23. 答案：(B)

英 ▶ 加

破 題 Where/should/I/put/box? ⇨ 問「地方」。

解 析 (A) 不對，Wh 問句不用 No 回答。(C) 此句為陷阱，題目中用 should（應該）即表示動作「還沒有」發生，此選項的 put 為過去式，不符合原句所問。(B) 的 corner 回答了重點，為正確答案。

錄音內容 Where should I put this box?
(A) No, I really shouldn't.
(B) In the corner would be fine.
(C) I think I put it on your desk.

錄音翻譯 我應該把這個箱子擺在哪裡？
(A) 不，我真的不應該。
(B) 擺在角落就可以了。
(C) 我想我是擺在你桌上。

24. 答案：(C)

澳 ▶ 英

破 題 Have/uniforms/come back...? ⇨ 問制服「是否」已取回。

解 析 (A) 答非所問，主詞不正確，重點應為 uniforms。(B) 用 Sure 表示「有」，但後半部句 how many... 則不知所云。(C) 先以 No 回應重點，接著以 be supposed to pick them up 來表示之後會去做。

錄音內容 Have the uniforms come back from the cleaners?
(A) We're required to wear a uniform at work.
(B) Sure, we can do that—how many are there?
(C) No, I'm supposed to go pick them up after five.

錄音翻譯 制服從洗衣店裡拿回來了嗎？
(A) 我們上班時必須穿制服。
(B) 當然，那點我們做得到──一共有多少個？
(C) 沒有，我要到五點以後才能去領。

□ uniform [ˋjunəfɔrm] *n.* 制服　　□ required [rɪˋkwaɪrd] *adj.* 必須的
□ cleaners [ˋklinəz] *n.* 乾洗店

25. 答案：(B)
澳▶美

破 題 What vehicle/you/need...? ⇨ 問需要「哪一種」交通工具。

解 析 (A) 答非所問。(C) 文不對題，Congratulations 與原句完全無關。(B) 用 I don't need 表「不需要」，用 one 表 vehicle；第二個句子則用來解釋不需要的原因，故為正確答案。

錄音內容 What vehicle do you need for tomorrow's job?
(A) Sure, go ahead, I won't need it.
(B) I don't need one. I will be working from here.
(C) Congratulations, when do you start?

錄音翻譯 你需要什麼交通工具去做明天的工作？
(A) 當然，拿去吧，我不需要。
(B) 我不需要交通工具。我會在這裡工作。
(C) 恭喜，你什麼時候開始？

☐ vehicle [ˋviɪkl] *n.* 運輸工具

26. 答案：(C)
英▶加

破 題 I'm/afraid/flight/delayed ⇨ 直述句，要了解說話者的意圖。

解 析 (A) 用字錯誤，原句 afraid 及 delayed 皆為負面字眼，不應用 happy 來回應。(B) 聯想錯誤，聽到 flight，可能會想到 seat，但 seat 與原句無關。(C) 前半句回應了重點，而 the weather's been bad 則解釋 not surprised 的原因。

錄音內容 I'm afraid the flight is going to be delayed an hour.
(A) Okay, I'll be happy to check for you.
(B) I'd really rather have an aisle seat, if that's possible.
(C) I'm not surprised; the weather's been bad.

錄音翻譯 恐怕班機會延誤一小時。
(A) 好，我很樂意去幫你看看。
(B) 假如可能的話，我真的寧願坐走道旁的位子。
(C) 我不意外；天氣一直都不好。

☐ flight [flaɪt] *n.* 班機
☐ delay [dɪˋle] *v.* 延遲

☐ aisle [aɪl] seat　靠走道座位
　（⟷ window seat　靠窗座位）

Test 1

Part

1

Part

2

Part

3

Part

4

Test 2

Part

1

Part

2

Part

3

Part

4

簡

答

27. 答案：(C)

澳 ▶ 加

破 題 How about...? ⇨ 表「建議」，要回答「接受」或「不接受」。

解 析 (A) 答非所問，November 表「時間」，與問句無關。(B) 不知所云，用 Yes 即為錯誤。(C) 用 where 指原句的 Conference Room B，而 it 指 interview，故為正確答案。

錄音內容 How about doing the interview in Conference Room B?
(A) The conference is in November.
(B) Yes, I'm here for my interview.
(C) That's where I was thinking of doing it.

錄音翻譯 在 B 會議室做面試怎麼樣？
(A) 會議在十一月舉行。
(B) 是的，我是來這裡面試。
(C) 我正想在那裡進行。

☐ conference room 會議室

28. 答案：(A)

英 ▶ 美

破 題 Where/find/deal/laptop? ⇨ 問「地方」。

解 析 (A) 用 I'd try 表「建議」，而 online 為尋找之「地方」，故為正確答案。(B) 時態錯誤。(C) Wh 問句不可用 No 回答。

錄音內容 Where can I find a good deal on a new laptop computer?
(A) I'd try searching online.
(B) I was thinking of buying one.
(C) No, mine has been working fine.

錄音翻譯 我可以在哪裡找到划算的新膝上型電腦？
(A) 我會試著上網搜尋。
(B) 我正在考慮買一台。
(C) 不，我的運作良好。

☐ deal [dil] *n.* 買賣   ☐ laptop computer 膝上（筆記）型電腦

29. 答案：(B)

英▶美

破 題 Should/I/dress/formally or casually? ⇨ 選擇性問句，要回答選擇「前者」或「後者」。

解 析 (A) 有 or 的問句，不可以用 Yes 或 No 回應。(C) 答非所問，in stock（有現貨）與問題無關。(B) 的 I would 表「意願」，而 formally 則為二選一之中的答案，為合理回應。

錄音內容 Should I dress formally or casually?
(A) Yes, that's probably best.
(B) I would dress formally.
(C) Let me see if that's in stock.

錄音翻譯 我應該穿著正式還是休閒服裝？
(A) 對，那大概是最好的。
(B) 我會穿得很正式。
(C) 我來看看那有沒有現貨。

□ dress [drɛs] *v.* 穿衣　　　　　　　□ casually [ˋkæʒjuəlɪ] *adv.* 休閒地
□ formally [ˋfɔrmlɪ] *adv.* 正式地　　□ in stock 有現貨的

30. 答案：(C)

加▶澳

破 題 Would it be okay if...? ⇨ 問「是否可以……」。

解 析 (A) 文法錯誤，didn't 為過去式。(B) 的 didn't 不但文法錯誤，且借題目重點字 comments 混淆視聽。(C) 的 Sure 表可以，as long as 表有但書，對應了題目中的 if，them 則指 comments，故為正解。

錄音內容 Would it be okay if I write my comments in the margins?
(A) No, I didn't put them there.
(B) I didn't have too many comments.
(C) Sure, as long as I can read them.

錄音翻譯 我把意見寫在邊緣可以嗎？
(A) 沒有，我沒有把它們放在那裡。
(B) 我沒有太多的意見。
(C) 當然可以，只要我可以讀就行。

□ comment [ˋkɑmənt] *n.* 評註　　　□ as long as 只要
□ margin [ˋmɑrdʒɪn] *n.* 邊緣

Test 1
Part 1
Part 2
Part 3
Part 4
Test 2
Part 1
Part 2
Part 3
Part 4
簡
答

31. 答案：(A)　　　　　　　　　　　　　英▶美

破題 Has/anyone/signed/nightshift? ➪ 問「有沒有人」上晚班。

解析 (A) 的 I think 表自己的看法，而 Susan 則代表了有人，故為正解。(B) midnight to six 答非所問，題目未問時間。(C) 不知所云，Thanks 及 appreciate 皆無法呼應原問句。

錄音內容 Has anyone signed up for the night shift?
(A) I think Susan has.
(B) From midnight to six.
(C) Thanks, I appreciate it.

錄音翻譯 有任何人簽名願意做晚班嗎？
(A) 我想蘇珊簽了。
(B) 從午夜到六點。
(C) 謝謝，我很感激。

□ sign up 簽字報名　　　　　　　　□ night shift [ʃɪft] 晚班
□ midnight [ˈmɪd.naɪt] *n.* 午夜　　　（⟷ day shift 早班；白天班）

32. 答案：(C)　　　　　　　　　　　　　澳▶美

破題 Is/entrance/route twenty/closed ➪ 問「是不是」。

解析 (A) 答非所問，問題中並沒做任何比較，故 best 不對。(B) 文不對題，不知所云。(C) 中的 It 指 route twenty，而 is supposed to open 和 after the weekend 則表示了目前仍是 closed，故為正確答案。

錄音內容 Is the entrance to route twenty still closed?
(A) That's definitely the best route.
(B) No, I haven't. Can you tell me why?
(C) It's supposed to be open after the weekend.

錄音翻譯 通往二十號的入口是不是還關閉？
(A) 那絕對是最好的路線。
(B) 不，我沒有。你能告訴我為什麼嗎？
(C) 週末結束後應該就會開放了。

□ entrance [ˈɛntrəns] *n.* 入口　　　　□ definitely [ˈdɛfənɪtlɪ] *adv.* 明顯地
□ route [rut] *n.* 路線

33. 答案：(C)

英▸澳

破　題 There should.../shouldn't there? ⇨ 考直述句 + 附加問句，故要回答「有」或「沒有」。

解　析 (A) 主詞 I 錯誤，原句中並沒有人稱字眼。(B) 文法錯誤，are 應改為 should。(C) Yes 及 there should 回答了題目重點，為正確答案。

錄音內容 There should be a bigger penalty for drunk driving, shouldn't there?
(A) Yes, I have.
(B) Yes, there are.
(C) Yes, there should.

錄音翻譯 酒醉駕車應該要罰得更重才對，不是嗎？
(A) 對，我有。
(B) 對，有。
(C) 對，應該。

□ penalty [ˈpɛnḷtɪ] *n.* 罰款　　　　□ drunk driving　酒醉駕車

34. 答案：(A)

澳▸加

破　題 Could/you/ask/Jenn/come/here? ⇨ 問「可否」請 Jenny 進來。

解　析 (A) I'll call her 回應了問題重點，為正確答案。(B) 主詞錯誤，題目並沒有提到 everyone。(C) 不對，是被介紹認識時說的話。

錄音內容 Could you please ask Jenny to come in here?
(A) I'll call her right now.
(B) Good, then everyone's here.
(C) Hi Jenny, it's nice to meet you.

錄音翻譯 可不可以麻煩你請珍妮進到這裡來？
(A) 我立刻打電話給她。
(B) 好，到時候大家都會來。
(C) 嗨，珍妮，幸會。

Test 1

Part
1

Part
2

Part
3

Part
4

Test 2

Part
1

Part
2

Part
3

Part
4

簡

答

35. 答案：(A)

破 題 When/magazine/subscription/expire? ⇨ 問雜誌訂閱期滿「時間」。

解 析 (A) Not until 表「直到……才……」，而 the end of the year 回答了題目重點，為正確答案。(B) 答非所問，不知所云。(C) 錯誤，Wh 開頭問句不可用 No 回應。

錄音內容 When does your magazine subscription expire?
(A) Not until the end of the year.
(B) I've been very happy with it.
(C) No thanks, I'm not interested.

錄音翻譯 你訂的雜誌什麼時候到期？
(A) 到明年底。
(B) 我對它十分滿意。
(C) 不用，謝謝，我沒興趣。

☐ subscription [səb`skrɪpʃən] *n.* 訂閱　　☐ expire [ɪk`spaɪr] *v.* （期限）終止；到期

36. 答案：(B)

破 題 Couldn't we/push/meeting back...? ⇨「否定問句」，要回答「可」或「不可」。

解 析 (A) 文法錯誤，was hoping 為過去進行式，而原句用 Could 表「客氣」，非過去式。(C) 答非所問，five of us 表人數，與原句毫無關聯。(B) 用 afraid 代表不能，回應了題目，故為正解。

錄音內容 Couldn't we push our meeting back to four?
(A) Too bad, I was hoping we could.
(B) I'm afraid I have a meeting then.
(C) There are five of us altogether.

錄音翻譯 我們不能把我們的會議延後到四點？
(A) 太糟了，我原本希望我們可以的。
(B) 恐怕我那個時候要開會。
(C) 我們總共有五個人。

☐ push back to 把……向後　　☐ altogether [ˌɔltə`gɛðə] *adv.* 全部

37. 答案：(C)　　　　　　　　　　　　　　　　　　　　英▶美

破題 What kind/work/you/get/with...? ⇨ 問「工作的種類」。

解析 (A) 提出了一不相關的問題，不知所云。(B) 答非所問，Wh 開頭的問句不用 No 來回答。(C) 的 Mostly academic work 則回應了重點，故完正確答案。

錄音內容 What kind of work can you get with a degree in Sociology?
(A) Where did you get that?
(B) No, I'm not finished yet.
(C) Mostly academic work, like teaching.

錄音翻譯 你靠社會學的學位可以找到哪種工作？
(A) 你是在哪裡弄到那個的？
(B) 不，我還沒做完。
(C) 主要是學術工作，像是教書。

☐ degree [dɪ`gri] *n.* 學位　　　　　　　☐ academic [ˌækə`dɛmɪk] *adj.* 學術的
☐ sociology [ˌsoʃɪ`alədʒɪ] *n.* 社會學

38. 答案：(B)　　　　　　　　　　　　　　　　　　　　澳▶美

破題 Do you want...? ⇨ 要回答「要」或「不要」。

解析 (A) 文法錯誤，haven't 應改為 don't。(C) 不對，應該是提問者下一句才會接的話。注意，Here you go. 是拿東西給人的常用句。(B) 的 I'd love something. 回應了重點，故為正確答案。

錄音內容 Do you want anything to drink?
(A) No, I haven't. How about you?
(B) I'd love something. What do you have?
(C) Here you go. Let me know if you want more.

錄音翻譯 你想不想喝點什麼？
(A) 不，我沒有。你呢？
(B) 我很想喝點東西。你有什麼？
(C) 拿去吧。你還要的話再告訴我。

☐ Here you go.　拿去吧。

Test 1

Part

1

Part

2

Part

3

Part

4

Test 2

Part

1

Part

2

Part

3

Part

4

39. 答案：(C)

英 ▶ 加

破題 What's happening...? ⇨ 問「發生了什麼事」。

解析 (A) 動詞錯誤，go out 與問題內容無關。(B) 用 easy to find 回答，卻不知所云。(C) 用 I'm not sure 回應了問題，雖不確定發生何事，不過 is loud 則說明了看法。

錄音內容 What's happening downstairs in the lobby?
(A) Okay, I'll go out the back.
(B) Oh, it's really easy to find.
(C) I'm not sure, but it sure is loud.

錄音翻譯 樓下的大廳發生了什麼事？
(A) 好，我會走後面出去。
(B) 喔，那真的很好找。
(C) 我不確定，不過還真吵。

☐ downstairs [ˋdaʊnˋstɛrz] *adv.* 在樓下

40. 答案：(B)

英 ▶ 澳

破題 We/have/enough paper/last...? ⇨「直述句」，說明紙夠用到月底。

解析 (A) 不知所云，Not yet 應用來回答「是否已經」的問句。(C) 答非所問，Look in the... drawer 表「在抽屜裡找」，與原句無關。(B) 的 I won't order 對應了直述句的重點，為正確答案。

錄音內容 We probably have enough paper to last for one month.
(A) Not yet. Do you have it with you?
(B) Then I won't order any more.
(C) Look in the top drawer in the cabinet.

錄音翻譯 我們的紙大概足夠用一個月。
(A) 還沒有。你身上有帶嗎？
(B) 那我就不再訂了。
(C) 看看櫃子最上面的抽屜。

☐ last [læst] *v.* 維持；夠用　　☐ cabinet [ˋkæbənɪt] *n.* 櫥；櫃
☐ top drawer 上層抽屜

41. 答案：(A)

破題 What/true/man ⇨ 聽取男子說與自己相關的「事實」字眼。

解析 男子在第一次發言時提到 ... my small business. I registered my business with the city...，故本題應選 (A)。

42. 答案：(B)

破題 What/woman/ask/man ⇨ 聽女子所問的「問題」。

解析 由女子第一次發言時提到的 Did you file a EM-one form with the city? 可知，本題應選 (B)。

43. 答案：(C)

破題 What/woman/remind/man/do ⇨ 聽取女子要男子做的「動作」字眼。

解析 由女子第二次發言時說的 ... remember to pay your quarterly tax estimates so... 可知，本題應選 (C)。注意，quarterly 即 every quarter。

録音内容

Questions 41 through 43 refer to the following conversation.

M: I have a question about my small business. I registered my business with the city in July. My question is, do I have to pay city taxes for the entire year?

W: Not at all. You only have to pay for the number of months you do business in the city. Did you file an EM-one form with the city?

M: My accountant put together all the paperwork. He's been in this city for something like thirty years, so I'm pretty sure he had me file all the necessary papers.

W: Good. Then remember to pay your quarterly tax estimates, so you're not assessed any penalties. If you registered in July, your first quarterly isn't due until September.

Test 1

Part 1

Part 2

Part 3

Part 4

Test 2

Part 1

Part 2

Part 3

Part 4

簡

答

録音翻譯

題目 41~43 請參照以下對話。

男：對於我的小企業，我有個問題。我在七月份向本市登記了我的企業，而我的問題是，我必須繳整年的市稅嗎？

女：不必，你只要付在市內做生意那幾個月的稅就行了。你有沒有向本市提出 EM-one 表？

男：我的會計師彙整了所有的書面文件。他在本市執業了三十年左右，所以我非常確定他幫我申報了所有的文件。

女：好。那要記得繳所估計的季稅，這樣就不會受到任何處罰。假如你是在七月登記，那第一季就是九月才到期。

題目 & 選項翻譯

41. 關於這位男子，何者為真？
    (A) 他開設了一家小企業。
    (B) 他未能準時繳稅。
    (C) 他是個執業會計師。
    (D) 他把他的企業遷到了新城市。

42. 女子問了男子什麼？
    (A) 他有沒有得到專業的稅務協助
    (B) 他有沒有向該市提出申報表格
    (C) 他在本市是否待了一年以上
    (D) 他有沒有估算自己應繳多少錢

43. 女子提醒男子要做什麼？
    (A) 繳罰款
    (B) 下個月回來
    (C) 每季繳稅
    (D) 九月時跟她的辦公室聯絡

- ☐ register [ˈrɛdʒɪstə] v. 註冊
- ☐ file [faɪl] v. 提出申請
- ☐ form [fɔrm] n. 表格
- ☐ accountant [əˈkaʊntənt] n. 會計師
- ☐ put together 組合；彙整
- ☐ paperwork [ˈpepəˌwɜk] n. 日常文書工作
- ☐ something like 大約 (= about)
- ☐ quarterly [ˈkwɔtəlɪ] adj. 按季的／adv. 按季地
- ☐ estimate [ˈɛstəˌmɪt] n. 估計；估計數

- ☐ assess [əˈsɛs] v. 徵（稅）；處（罰款）
- ☐ penalty [ˈpɛnˌltɪ] n. 罰款
- ☐ due [dju] adj. 到期的
- ☐ fail to do V 沒有能夠做……
- ☐ on time 準時
- ☐ certified [ˈsɜtəfaɪd] public accountant 有照會計師 (= CPA)
- ☐ relocate [riˈloket] v. 重新安置
- ☐ professional [prəˈfɛʃənl] adj. 專業的
- ☐ charge [tʃɑrdʒ] n. 費用；索價

Test 1

Part

1

Part

2

Part

3

Part

4

Test 2

Part

1

Part

2

Part

3

Part

4

簡

答

MP3
171 **Questions 44~46**   男：英 女：加

44. 答案：(D)

破題 What/man/do ⇨ 聽取男子或女子講男子所做的「動作」字眼。

解析 女子第一次發言時提到 You've <u>convinced</u> us to <u>go with</u> the... frame <u>assembly</u> for the <u>motor housing</u>.，而 You 即指男子，故應選 (D)。此處用 persuade 代替原句的 convinced，用 product 代替 leadless frame assembly。

45. 答案：(D)

破題 What/man/benefit/using/product ⇨ 聽取男子所說的「好處」字眼。

解析 男子第一次發言提到 ... you realized... <u>benefits</u>..., such as a <u>lighter</u> <u>weight</u> assembly, <u>better</u> heat conductivity，故應選 (D)。注意，比較級常為出題重點。

46. 答案：(A)

破題 How/man/assist ⇨ 聽取男子所說的協助「方法」。

解析 男子第二次發言提到 ... We can <u>also</u> <u>help</u> you <u>assemble</u> your first <u>frames</u>, if you wish，故應選 (A)。此處用 construction 來代替原句 assemble first frames。注意，also 在句中有「附加」資訊的概念，也常為出題重點。

録音内容

Questions 44 through 46 refer to the following conversation.

W: You've convinced us to go with the leadless frame assembly for the motor housing. The price is good, the fact that it's environmentally safer is great...

M: But hopefully, you realized there are performance benefits as well, such as a lighter weight assembly, better heat conductivity...

W: No, you convinced us, leadless is the way to go. Now, are there any guidelines you'd recommend, anything we need to know about?

M: National guidelines were published by the government, so we can direct you to those resources. We can also help you assemble your first frames, if you wish.

録音翻譯

題目 44~46 請參照以下對話。

女：你已說服我們在馬達外殼上採用無鉛框組。它的價格理想，對環境無害的事實也很棒……

男：不過但願妳明白，它也有性能上的好處，像是組合的重量比較輕、導熱性更好……

女：不，你說服我們無鉛是該走的路。現在你有沒有什麼要建議的準則，有什麼我們需要知道的事？

男：國家準則是由政府所發布的，所以我們可以告訴你們如何取得那些資源。假如妳希望的話，我們還可以幫你們組裝第一套框架。

題目 & 選項翻譯

44. 男子做了什麼？

(A) 提議降低產品價格

(B) 協助女子製造產品

(C) 讓女子暫時使用產品

(D) 說服女子購買產品

45. 男子說使用產品的好處之一是什麼？

(A) 用比較少的能源就能運作該產品。

(B) 該產品比較重又比較耐用。

(C) 組裝該產品時需要比較少的人力。

(D) 該產品不像其他類似的產品那麼重。

46. 男子提議要怎麼協助女子？

(A) 協助她建構

(B) 安排她取得政府許可

(C) 審視她的製造計畫

(D) 寫一套量身訂做的準則

- [ ] convince [kən`vɪns] v. 使信服
- [ ] go with 順從……的趨勢
- [ ] leadless [`lɛdlɪs] adj. 無鉛的
- [ ] frame [frem] n. 骨架；框架
- [ ] assembly [ə`sɛmblɪ] n.（機械的）裝配
- [ ] housing [`haʊzɪŋ] n.【機】外罩；箱
- [ ] environmentally [ɛn͵vaɪrən`mɛntlɪ] adv. 有關環境方面
- [ ] performance [pə`fɔrməns] n.（機械等）性能
- [ ] benefit [`bɛnəfɪt] n. 益處

- [ ] conductivity [͵kɑndʌk`tɪvətɪ] n.【物】傳導性
- [ ] guideline [`gaɪd͵laɪn] n. 指導方針
- [ ] recommend [͵rɛkə`mɛnd] v. 推薦
- [ ] assemble [ə`sɛmbl] v. 組裝
- [ ] temporary [`tɛmpə͵rɛrɪ] adj. 暫時的
- [ ] durable [`djʊrəbl] adj. 耐用的
- [ ] construction [kən`strʌkʃən] n. 建造
- [ ] permit [`pɝmɪt] n. 許可；執照
- [ ] customized [`kʌstə͵maɪzd] adj. 量身訂作的

Test 1
Part 1
Part 2
Part 3
Part 4
Test 2
Part 1
Part 2
Part 3
Part 4
簡答

MP3 172 Questions 47~49

男：美 女：加

47. 答案：(B)

破題 Where/conversation/take place ⇨ 聽取「地點」或與地點有關的屬性字眼，多為「名詞」。

解析 女子第一次發言提到 impressive <u>resume</u>... experience...，而聽到 resume 時，即可推知答案為 (B) job interview。

48. 答案：(A)

破題 What/learned/man ⇨ 聽取與「男子」有關的資訊。

解析 由男子在一次發言時提到的 I think my <u>major</u> experience... <u>management</u> and documentation. 可知，本題應選 (A)。注意，在 major 這類的特別字眼之後的資訊，常為出題重點。

49. 答案：(C)

破題 What/woman/ask/man/do ⇨ 聽取女子要男子做的「動作」字眼。

解析 女子第二次發言提到 When you say <u>documentation</u>, <u>you mean</u>...。一般而言，聽到句中有 you mean...，即表示希望對方將之前所說的事情釐清之意，故本題應選 (C)。

錄音內容

Questions 47 through 49 refer to the following conversation.

W: You have a very impressive resume—a lot of experience in the environmental services industry. Which area would you say you have the greatest experience in?

M: Management and documentation, definitely. I've worked in engineering and construction too, but I think my major experience has been management and documentation.

W: When you say documentation, you mean...

M: Umm, management plans, site analyses, quality-control, environmental protection... I've been in the industry eighteen years, so it really covers a lot.

Test 1

Part
1

Part
2

Part
3

Part
4

Test 2

Part
1

Part
2

Part
3

Part
4

簡
答

錄音翻譯

題目 47~49 請參照以下對話。

女：你的履歷非常精彩，在環境服務業的經驗豐富。你說你在哪個方面的經驗最豐富？

男：絕對是管理和文件方面。我也做過工程和營造，但我想我的主要經驗是管理和文件。

女：你所謂的文件是指⋯⋯

男：嗯，管理計畫、地點分析、品管、環保⋯⋯我已經在這行待十八年了，所以真的涵蓋很廣。

題目＆選項翻譯

47. 這段對話可能在哪裡出現？

    (A) 會議時

    (B) 工作面試時

    (C) 員工大會中

    (D) 接待區

48. 關於這名男子，我們得知什麼？

    (A) 他有過當經理的經驗。

    (B) 他專攻地點分析。

    (C) 他在工地工作。

    (D) 他擁有環境科學的學位。

49. 女子要男子做什麼？

    (A) 把文件交給她

    (B) 記錄他的進度

    (C) 釐清他提出的論點

    (D) 檢視她的營業計畫

☐ impressive [ɪm`prɛsɪv] *adj.* 令人印象深刻的

☐ resume [ˌrɛzjʊ`me] *n.* 履歷

☐ industry [`ɪndʌstrɪ] *n.* 產業

☐ documentation [ˌdɑkjəmɛn`teʃən] *n.* 文件；文獻

☐ definitely [`dɛfənɪtlɪ] *adv.* 明確地

☐ engineering construction 工程營造

☐ analysis [ə`næləsɪs] *n.* 分析

☐ reception [rɪ`sɛpʃən] *n.* 接待

☐ specialize in 專攻

☐ environmental science 環境科學

☐ hand [hænd] *v.* 面交；給

☐ clarify [`klærəˌfaɪ] *v.* 釐清

☐ business plan 營業計畫

MP3 173 Questions 50~52

男：美 女：澳

50. 答案：(D)

破題 What/man's problem ⇨ 聽取男子說的「問題」字眼 或「否定、負面」字眼。

解析 男子第一次發言說到 I had a <u>problem</u> with the <u>images</u> I <u>received</u> from Gary.，故本題應選 (D)。

51. 答案：(C)

破題 What/kind/work/speakers/doing ⇨ 聽取與兩人有關的「工作屬性」字眼。

解析 女子第二次發言時提到 <u>But</u> we're <u>not</u> going... <u>able</u> to <u>finalize</u> the <u>marketing</u> <u>plan</u> <u>until</u> they have a stable product.，故本題選 (C)。此處用 formulating 代替 able 及 finalize 的概念。注意，but 及 not... until 是聽力的指標字眼，常會有出題重點。

52. 答案：(B)

破題 What/woman/suggest/speakers/so ⇨ 聽取女子說「建議性」的動作字眼。

解析 由女子第二次發言時提到的 <u>We</u> can <u>continue</u> our <u>analysis</u>... 可知，本題應選 (B)。

（錄音內容）

Questions 50 through 52 refer to the following conversation.

M: I had a problem with the images I received from Gary. They all had this problem with text—the text sizes kept changing from screen to screen. Did you see that?

W: Yes, I did. I think what they're doing is taking shots of the computer screen, and then changing the software, which of course changes the screen.

M: Ahh, that would explain the text size changing all over the place. Okay, so the question is, when do you think they'll have a final product, at least as far as the main screens are concerned?

W: I don't know. We can continue our analysis in the meantime—it won't be affected by the software delay. But we're not going to be able to finalize the marketing plan until they have a stable product.

Test 1

Part

1

Part

2

Part

3

Part

4

Test 2

Part

1

Part

2

Part

3

Part

4

簡

答

錄音翻譯

題目 50~52 請參照以下對話。

男：我從蓋瑞那裡收到的影像有個問題。它們的文字都有同樣的問題——文字大小一直隨畫面改變。妳有沒有看到？

女：有，我看到了。我想他們的做法是拍攝電腦螢幕，然後改變軟體，所以當然會改變畫面。

男：啊，那就能解釋文字大小在各個地方的改變了。好，所以問題是，妳認為他們什麼時候會做出最終產品，起碼是在主畫面的部分。

女：我不曉得。在此同時我們可以繼續我們的分析——它不會受到軟體延誤的影響。可是我們得等到他們做出穩定的產品後，才能敲定行銷計畫。

題目&選項翻譯

50. 男子的問題是什麼？
    (A) 他的電腦無法正常運作。
    (B) 他看不到畫面上的內文。
    (C) 客戶沒有回答他的問題。
    (D) 他收到的檔案有問題。

51. 說話者很可能在做什麼工作？
    (A) 寫純文字文件
    (B) 拍攝產品照片
    (C) 擬訂行銷計畫
    (D) 開發電腦程式

52. 女子建議說話者做什麼？
    (A) 改變他們的策略
    (B) 繼續做他們的工作
    (C) 立刻完成他們的工作
    (D) 盡快聯絡蓋瑞

☐ on-screen [ˈɑnˈskrin] *adj.* 螢幕上的
☐ formulate [ˈfɔrmjəˌlet] *v.* 規劃（制度、計畫等）
☐ strategy [ˈstrætədʒɪ] *n.* 策略
☐ immediately [ɪˈmidɪɪtlɪ] *adv.* 立刻
☐ contact [ˈkɑntækt] *n.* 合約

Questions 53~55

男：美 女：加

53. 答案：(A)

破 題 What/man's problem ⇨ 聽取男子的「問題」或「否定、負面」字眼。

解 析 男子第一次發言提到 I was <u>wondering why</u> I <u>hadn't</u> been <u>paid</u> for the <u>third</u>。wondering why 後即接問題字眼，故本題應選 (A)。

54. 答案：(B)

破 題 What/information/man/give/woman ⇨ 注意聽男子說的資訊，通常重點字為名詞，或名詞與動詞之結合。

解 析 由男子第二次發言時提到的 I <u>received</u> a <u>payment</u> on <u>invoice number</u>... 可知，本題應選 (B)。注意，數字常為出題關鍵。

55. 答案：(A)

破 題 what/woman/claim/done ⇨ 聽取女子說她「做過的事情」。

解 析 女子第二次發言時提到的 According to my records, all three checks were mailed out... 可知，本題正確答案為 (A)。

(錄音內容)

Questions 53 through 55 refer to the following conversation.

M: I received a check for two of the three projects you owed me money on. I was wondering why I hadn't been paid for the third.

W: Okay, let me check... Okay, I have you being owed for three contracts that were completed between May and June. Is that right?

M: That's right. I received payment on invoice number one-oh-eight-five, and one-oh-eight-seven, but not one-oh-eight-six.

W: According to my records, all three checks were mailed out at the same time. If you only received two of them, the problem is with the mail. I would give it another couple of days.

Test 1

Part

1

Part

2

Part

3

Part

4

Test 2

Part

1

Part

2

Part

3

Part

4

簡

答

録音翻譯

題目 53~55 請參照以下對話。

男：你們欠我款項的三個案子，我只收到了兩個案子的支票。我在想我為什麼沒有拿到第三個案子的款項？

女：好，我來查查看……好，我看到您有三個合約的欠款沒拿到，合約完成時間是在五、六月之間。這樣對嗎？

男：沒錯，我收到付款的發票號碼是 1085 和 1087，但沒有 1086。

女：根據我的記錄，這三張支票是同時寄出的。假如您只收到其中兩張，問題就出在郵寄上了。我會再等幾天看看。

題目&選項翻譯

53. 男子的問題是什麼？
    (A) 他做的一項工作沒有拿到錢。
    (B) 他找不到他所收到的支票。
    (C) 他把發票寄錯了地址。
    (D) 他給錯了聯絡方式。

54. 男子給了女子什麼資訊？
    (A) 他的電話號碼
    (B) 他的發票號碼
    (C) 他的服務價格
    (D) 他完成工作的日期

55. 女子表示已經做了什麼？
    (A) 郵寄支票
    (B) 簽約
    (C) 忘了寄錢
    (D) 記錯金額

☐ check [tʃɛk] *n.* 支票　　　　　☐ invoice [ˋɪnvɔɪs] *n.* 發票
☐ complete [kəmˋplit] *v.* 完成　　☐ according to 根據
☐ payment [ˋpemənt] *n.* 付款　　☐ sign [saɪn] *v.* 簽約

Questions 56~58   男：英 女：澳

56. 答案：(C)

破題 What/speakers discussing ⇨ 考「主旨」，注意聽重點「名詞」。

解析 女子第一次發言提到 The question isn't whether we can <u>design</u> the <u>annual report</u>..., the question is whether <u>it's</u> the best choice...。其中的 it 指的就是 design the <u>annual report</u>，說話者一直重覆的名詞即為重點，因此判斷 (C) 為正確答案。

57. 答案：(A)

破題 What/speakers/disagree ⇨ 聽二者「意見不同」的內容，注意「負面、否定」字眼。

解析 由女子第二次發言時說的 I'm <u>not</u> <u>certain</u> we're interested in <u>becoming</u> a <u>design firm</u>. 來推斷，正確答案為 (A)。此處以 whether、should do 來代替原句的 not certain... become...。

58. 答案：(B)

破題 What/man/say/speaker's decision ⇨ 聽取男子對於決定的「看法或評論」。

解析 男子第一次發言時提到 My reasoning is this: we're going to learn from this job. It's a <u>low-risk venture</u>...，故應選（B）。此處用 not involve a lot of risk 代替原句的 low-risk venture。

（錄音內容）

Questions 56 through 58 refer to the following conversation.

W: The question isn't whether we CAN design the annual report ourselves, the question is whether it's the best choice for us. I'm not sure we're going to end up saving that much money, once all's said and done.

M: I think we should give it a go. My reasoning is this: we're going to learn from this job. It's a low-risk venture—if we don't do it well, very few people are going to be impacted. And by doing it, we'll pick up skills we didn't have before.

W: Okay, those are good points. But these skills are only worth picking up if we want to do this kind of work again. I'm not certain we're interested in becoming a design firm.

M: Well, if we have the skills, who knows? Maybe we might end up adding that kind of work to our skill set.

Test 1

Part 1

Part 2

Part 3

Part 4

Test 2

Part 1

Part 2

Part 3

Part 4

簡

答

錄音翻譯

題目 56~58 請參照以下對話。

女：問題不在於我們能不能自行設計年報，問題在於它是不是我們的最佳選擇。總歸一句話，我不確定我們最後能省下那麼多的錢。

男：我想我們應該試試看。我的道理是：我們會從這項工作中學到東西。這是個低風險的做法，假如我們做得不好，會受到影響的人也很少。而且這麼做可以讓我們學到以前所缺乏的技巧。

女：好，這些論點不錯。可是只有當我們想把這些工作再做一次時，這些技巧才值得學。我不確定我們會對成為一家設計公司感興趣。

男：嗯，假如我們有了這些技巧，誰知道呢？也許我們最後會把那種工作變成我們的技術之一。

題目 & 選項翻譯

56. 說話者在討論什麼？
(A) 營業計畫
(B) 公司標誌
(C) 年報
(D) 產品設計

57. 說話者對什麼事意見不同？
(A) 他們是否該做某樣工作
(B) 他們應該在何時展開工作
(C) 他們應該花多少錢
(D) 他們應該雇用誰來做這項工作

58. 對於說話者的決定，男子說了什麼？
(A) 不應該太快下決定。
(B) 情況不會有太多風險。
(C) 應該找更多人來參與決定。
(D) 在決定前應該做更多工作。

- [ ] annual report 年報
- [ ] end up + Ving 以………收場
- [ ] once all's said and done 塵埃落定
- [ ] give it a go 姑且一試
- [ ] reasoning [ˋriznɪŋ] *n.* 推論

- [ ] venture [ˋvɛntʃɚ] *n.* 冒險事業
- [ ] impact [ɪmˋpækt] *v.* 對……產生影響
- [ ] corporate [ˋkɔrpərɪt] *adj.* 公司的
- [ ] be involved in 涉入

Test 1

Part
1

Part
2

Part
3

Part
4

Test 2

Part
1

Part
2

Part
3

Part
4

簡

答

MP3
176 **Questions 59~61**　　　　　　　　男：英　女：加

59. 答案：(D)

破題 What/man/say/benefit/museum/membership ⇨ 聽取男子說關於 museum membership 的「好處」字眼。

解析 男子第二次發言時提到 We get <u>free</u> <u>entry</u> to the museum and we <u>also</u> get <u>discounts</u> to... <u>shops</u> and <u>restaurants</u>.，故本題應選 (D)。注意，free entry 並不包括其他人，故 (B) 不對。

60. 答案：(D)

破題 What/man/say/membership/purchase ⇨ 注意聽與 purchase 有關的句子。

解析 男子第二次發言提到 ... a <u>museum</u> <u>saleman</u> <u>called</u>, ... asked me to <u>join</u>... but it <u>sounds</u> really <u>cool</u>.，it 即指「加入成為會員」這件事，故本題應選 (D)。

61. 答案：(B)

破題 What/true/speakers ⇨ 聽取二者的「共同點」或「關連性」字眼。

解析 男子第一次發言提到的 <u>You</u>, <u>me</u> and the <u>kids</u>. 及女子第二次發言提到的... we're going to start taking <u>family trips</u> to the museum... 中皆有表二者「關係」的字眼，二者明顯是一家人，故本題應選 (B)。

錄音內容

Questions 59 through 61 refer to the following conversation.

M: I bought us a membership to the science museum today. You, me, and the kids.

W: That's an odd thing to do. Did you happen to be at the museum today?

M: No, a museum salesman called, gave me his pitch, and asked me to join. I know, it was impulsive but it sounds really cool. We get free entry to the museum, and we also get discounts to other participating shops and restaurants.

W: Oh, it's fine with me, just unexpected. I guess we're going to start taking family trips to the museum then, eh?

錄音翻譯

題目 59~61 請參照以下對話。

男：我今天幫咱們大家買了科學博物館的會員資格。你、我，還有孩子們。

女：這麼做真怪。你今天是剛好去博物館嗎？

男：不是，博物館的業務員打電話來，對我推銷了一番，並要我加入。我知道這是一時衝動，但聽起來真的很棒。我們可以免費進入博物館，而且到其他的聯名商店和餐廳還能打折。

女：哦，我是無所謂，只是覺得很突然。我想以後我們要開始全家去逛博物館了，是吧？

題目&選項翻譯

59. 男子說博物館的會員資格有什麼好處？
   (A) 免費停車
   (B) 帶客人可免費進入
   (C) 受邀參加特別活動
   (D) 在某些餐廳有打折

60. 對於他所買的會員資格，男子說了什麼？
   (A) 他是買來當作禮物的。
   (B) 他是在博物館時買的。
   (C) 他計畫很久了。
   (D) 他是聽了電話銷售人員的話。

61. 關於說話者，何者可能為真？
   (A) 他們工作的對象是小孩。
   (B) 他們住在同一戶。
   (C) 他們倆都對科學感興趣。
   (D) 他們隸屬專業組織。

□ membership [`mɛnbə.ʃɪp] *n.* 會員資格
□ odd [ad] *adj.* 奇特的
□ impulsive [ɪm`pʌlsɪv] *adj.* 衝動的
□ entry [`ɛntrɪ] *n.* 入場
□ participating [par`tɪsə.petɪŋ] *adj.* 參與的；分享的
□ unexpected [ʌnɪk`spɛktɪd] *adj.* 無預期的
□ regarding [rɪ`gardɪŋ] *prep.* 關於
□ purchase [`pɝtʃəs] *n./v.* 購買
□ household [`haʊs.hold] *n.* 一家人；戶
□ belong to 隸屬；是……的成員
□ organization [.ɔrgənə`zeʃən] *n.* 組織

Test 1
Part
1
Part
2
Part
3
Part
4
Test 2
Part
1
Part
2
Part
3
Part
4
簡
答

MP3 177 **Questions 62~64** 男：美 女：澳

62. 答案：(D)

破題 What/did/man/do ⇨ 聽取男子過去做的「動作」字眼。

解析 男子第一次發言提到 ... I <u>wasn't</u> <u>planning</u> on <u>going</u>. It's a tradeoff...，故本
題應選(D)。此處用 change his mind 代替原句的 not planning on going。

63. 答案：(A)

破題 What/man/concerned ⇨ 聽取男子說的「疑問」或「負面」字眼。

解析 男子第一次發言提到 ... every time I travel, I <u>miss</u> some <u>sales</u> at home. I
was <u>afraid</u> the lost <u>sales</u> <u>opportunities</u>...，故本題應選 (A)。

64. 答案：(C)

破題 What/man/plan/do ⇨ 聽取男子「未來」會做的「動作」字眼。

解析 男子第二次發言提到 ... I'm <u>going</u> to <u>meet</u> with <u>them</u>, <u>visit</u> their offices.，
這裡的 them 指的就是上一句中的 clients，故本題應選 (C)。

録音內容

Questions 62 through 64 refer to the following conversation.

W: So you decided to attend the trade show in San Antonio after all. I thought
you weren't planning on doing it.

M: You're right, I wasn't planning on going. It's a tradeoff—every time I travel,
I miss some sales at home. I was afraid the lost sales opportunities were
going to outweigh the benefits.

W: So what made you change your mind?

M: The fact that we have some clients in San Antonio. I'm going to meet with
them, visit their offices. It's a chance to have some face-to-face time—that,
plus the trade show makes the trip worthwhile.

録音翻譯

題目 62~64 請參照以下對話。

女：所以你終究決定要去參加聖安東尼奧的商展。我以為你不打算這麼做。

男：妳說得對，我本來沒打算去。這是一個權衡——每次我出差，就會錯過一些本地的生意。我怕失去的商機比好處還大。

女：那什麼讓你改變了心意？

男：因為我們在聖安東尼奧有一些客戶。我要去見他們，到他們的辦公室看看。這是個讓人有一些面對面時間的機會，而這點加上商展就使這趟值得一去。

題目 & 選項翻譯

62. 男子做了什麼？

(A) 參加商展

(B) 更改預訂班機

(C) 完成會議登記

(D) 改變心意要出席一項活動

63. 男子擔心什麼？

(A) 失去生意

(B) 出差旅行安全

(C) 花太多錢

(D) 喪失工作福利

64. 男子說他打算做什麼？

(A) 回家

(B) 待在辦公室

(C) 跟客戶見面

(D) 找家便宜的旅館

- ☐ trade show 商展
- ☐ after all 畢竟；到底
- ☐ tradeoff [ˈtrɛdˌɔf] *n.* 權衡
- ☐ opportunity [ˌɑpɚˈtjunətɪ] *n.* 機會
- ☐ outweigh [ˌaʊtˈwe] *v.* 比……重要
- ☐ client [ˈklaɪənt] *n.* 客戶

- ☐ face-to-face [ˈfɛstəˈfes] *adj.* 面對面的
- ☐ worthwhile [ˈwɝθˈhwaɪl] *adj.* 值得（花時間和金錢）做的
- ☐ reservation [ˌrɛzɚˈveʃən] *n.* 預訂（的房間或席位）
- ☐ registration [ˌrɛdʒɪˈstreʃən] *n.* 登記

Test 1
Part 1
Part 2
Part 3
Part 4
Test 2
Part 1
Part 2
Part 3
Part 4
簡 答

MP3 178 **Questions 65~67**　　　　　　男：美　女：加

65. 答案：(A)

[破 題] what/learned/man's company ⇨ 注意聽男子或女子談到與「男子公司」相關的字眼。

[解 析] 由女子第一次發言提到 G-B-C has become the largest... bank in Vietnam, and... largest in... Asia. 以及男子第二次發言說的 These techniques are common in the West, but... we adopted them... 可推斷，正確答案為 (A)。

66. 答案：(C)

[破 題] What/woman/imply/man's company ⇨ 注意聽女子說男子公司的相關事情。

[解 析] 女子第二次發言時提到 But plenty of banks have opened in Vietnam... How have you managed to beat the competition?，由此可推斷正確答案為 (C)。此處的 local 指的就是在 Vietnam。

67. 答案：(B)

[破 題] What/reason/man/give/company's success ⇨ 聽男子說「原因、理由」字眼。

[解 析] 男子第二次發言提到 We learned a lot from outside banks—thing like...，故本題應選 (B)。

[錄音內容]

Questions 65 through 67 refer to the following conversation.

W: In the past ten years, G-B-C has become the largest private commercial bank in Vietnam, and one of the largest in all of Asia. How have you accomplished this?

M: Some of it was timing. Vietnam has had a booming economy for the last ten years. It's had a lot to do with our success.

W: But plenty of other banks have opened in Vietnam during the same period. How have you managed to beat the competition?

M: We learned a lot from outside banks—things like loan application approvals, data centralization. These techniques are common in the West, but they were innovative when we adopted them in Vietnam.

(錄音翻譯)

題目 65~67 請參照以下對話。

女：過去十年來，GBC 已經成為越南最大的私人商業銀行，在全亞洲也名列前茅。你們是怎麼做到這點的？

男：部分原因在於時機。越南在過去十年間的經濟蒸蒸日上，這跟我們的成功有很大的關係。

女：可是在同一段期間，很多其他的銀行也在越南成立。你們是靠什麼辦法打敗競爭對手的？

男：我們向外面的銀行學了很多，像是核准申請貸款、資料集中等等。這些技術在西方很普遍，但是當我們在越南採用時卻是項創新。

(題目&選項翻譯)

65. 關於這名男子的公司，我們得知什麼？
    (A) 它的總部位在亞洲。
    (B) 它在世界各地都有辦事處。
    (C) 它是在經濟低迷時開辦。
    (D) 它營業還不到十個月。

66. 對於男子的公司，女子暗示了什麼？
    (A) 它借了很多錢。
    (B) 它需要繼續創新。
    (C) 它在當地面臨了很大的競爭。
    (D) 它強勁的經濟表現可能不會持久。

67. 男子說公司成功的原因是什麼？
    (A) 有最優秀的管理階層。
    (B) 向其他公司學習。
    (C) 得利於新科技。
    (D) 草創時資金充裕。

- [ ] commercial bank 商業銀行
- [ ] accomplish [əˋkamplɪʃ] v. 實現
- [ ] booming [ˋbumɪŋ] adj. 繁榮的；景氣好的
- [ ] have a lot to do with 與……密切相關（⟷ have nothing to do with 與……毫無關聯）
- [ ] beat [bit] v. 打敗
- [ ] competition [ˌkampəˋtɪʃən] n. 競爭
- [ ] application [ˌæpləˋkeʃən] n. 申請
- [ ] approval [əˋpruvl] n. 核准；認可

- [ ] centralization [ˌsɛntrəlɪˋzeʃən] n. 集中化
- [ ] innovative [ˋɪnəˌvetɪv] adj. 創新的
- [ ] adopt [əˋdapt] v. 採用
- [ ] headquarter [ˋhɛdˌkwɔrtə] v.【口】設立總部
- [ ] downturn [ˋdaʊnˌtɜn] n.（經濟）衰退
- [ ] be in business 營業
- [ ] face [fes] v. 面對
- [ ] well-funded [ˋwɛlˋfʌdɪd] adj. 資金充裕的
- [ ] start out 出發

Questions 68~70

男：美　女：澳

68. 答案：(D)

（破題）What/man/probably/doing ➡ 聽取男子說目前正在做的「動作」字眼。

（解析）由男子第一次發言提到的 Your <u>price</u> are... <u>lower</u> than... other jewelers. 以及第二次發言提到 <u>But</u> you <u>use</u> pure platinum? <u>I mean</u> when I <u>purchase</u> ... 可推知，正確答案為 (D)。

69. 答案：(C)

（破題）What/woman/say/her business ➡ 聽取女子談論自己企業的相關字句。

（解析）由女子第一次發言時提到的 <u>Remember</u>, we're <u>manufacturers</u>, not just retails. 可知，本題應選 (C)。此處用 manufactures its own products 來代替原句的 manufacturers。

70. 答案：(B)

（破題）What/man/concerned ➡ 聽取男子說的「疑問」或「負面、否定」字眼。

（解析）由男子第二次發言 <u>I mean</u>, when I <u>purchase</u>... I can be <u>sure</u> it's <u>one-hundred percent</u> platinum? 可知，本題應選 (B)。此處用 The purity of the materials used 代替原句的 one-hundred percent platinum。

（錄音內容）

Questions 68 through 70 refer to the following conversation.

M: Your prices are significantly lower than the other jewelers. How do you manage that, without sacrificing quality?

W: First of all, you can't compare us to other jewelry retailers. Remember, we're manufacturers, not just retailers. When you buy from us, you're buying directly from the manufacturer.

M: But you use pure platinum? I mean, when I purchase a watch or pendant, I can be sure it's one-hundred percent platinum?

W: Absolutely! Pure platinum is just that: one hundred percent pure. Additional minerals may be added to some pieces, but those pieces are not labeled as being pure.

題目 68~70 請參照以下對話。

男：你們的價格遠低於其他珠寶業者。你們是怎麼做到這點又不會犧牲品質的？

女：首先，你不能拿我們跟其他的珠寶零售商相提並論。記住，我們是製造商，而不只是零售商。當你跟我們買東西時，你是直接跟製造商買。

男：可是你們用的是純白金嗎？我是說，當我買錶或吊飾時，我可以確定它是百分之百的白金嗎？

女：當然！純白金就是如此：百分之百的純。有些東西可能會加入其他的礦物，但是那些東西就不會標示為純。

68. 男子可能在做什麼？
    (A) 確認之前的協議
    (B) 談判長期的銷售合約
    (C) 研究設法把一項設計製造出來
    (D) 決定要不要買女子的產品

69. 對於她的企業，女子說了什麼？
    (A) 它的生意比競爭對手的好。
    (B) 它分銷國際。
    (C) 它自行製造產品。
    (D) 它只賣給零售大眾。

70. 男子擔心什麼事？
    (A) 產品的價格
    (B) 所用材料的純度
    (C) 製造的品質
    (D) 公司的長期穩定度

- ☐ significantly [sɪg`nɪfəkəntlɪ] *adv.* 意味深長地；重大的
- ☐ jeweler [`dʒuələ] *n.* 珠寶商
- ☐ sacrifice [`sækrə͵faɪs] *v.* 犧牲
- ☐ first of all 首先
- ☐ retailer [`ritelə] *n.* 零售商
- ☐ manufacturer [͵mænjə`fæktʃərə] *n.* 製造商
- ☐ platinum [`plætŋəm] *n.* 白金
- ☐ pendant [`pɛndənt] *n.* 垂飾
- ☐ absolutely [`æbsə͵lutlɪ] *adv.* 完全地
- ☐ mineral [`mɪnərəl] *n.* 礦物
- ☐ previous [`privɪəs] *adj.* 先前的
- ☐ negotiate [nɪ`goʃɪͺet] *v.* 協商
- ☐ long-term [`lɔŋ͵tɝm] *adj.* 長期的
- ☐ look into 深入地檢查
- ☐ outsell [͵aut`sɛl] *v.* 賣得比……多
- ☐ distribute [dɪ`strɪbjut] *v.* 分銷
- ☐ internationally [͵ɪntə`næʃənͺlɪ] *adv.* 國際地
- ☐ purity [`pjurətɪ] *n.* 純度
- ☐ stability [stə`bɪlətɪ] *n.* 穩定度
- ☐ label [`lebl̩] *v.* 標示

Test 1
Part 1
Part 2
Part 3
Part 4
Test 2
Part 1
Part 2
Part 3
Part 4
簡答

Part ④

MP3 181 **Questions 71~73** 美

71. 答案：(B)

破題 Where/man/posted/resume ⇨ 聽取男子講與 resume 有關的「地點」字眼。

解析 第一行提到 ... posted... resume online，第四行提到 ... I decided to post my resume on a couple of internet job sites.，可知答案為 (B)。

72. 答案：(C)

破題 What/man/do/before/posting ⇨ 聽取男子先說的「動作」字眼。

解析 第二句提到 ... but I really thought... 表「先前的動作」，故聽到 the best strategy was to find the job opening and then e-mail my resume to H-R office... 時，即可知答案為 (C)。

73. 答案：(B)

破題 What/man/indicate/result/posting ⇨ 聽取表「結果」之「動作」字眼。

解析 第五、六行的 Well, I tell you what，表示要告訴對方「結果」，故之後的 I posted my account..., and I was already getting phone calls from recruiters. 即為答案，故本題應選 (B)。

(錄音內容)

Questions 71 through 73 refer to the following talk.

I wasn't sure, when I posted my resume online, that it was really going to lead to any job offers. I mean, I already used the Internet to search for jobs, but I really thought the best strategy was to find the job openings and then e-mail my resume to the H-R office, or whatever. But since I wasn't having any luck, I decided to post my resume on a couple of Internet job sites. Well, I'll tell you what, I posted my account on Monday, and by Wednesday I was already getting phone calls from recruiters. It would have taken me weeks to get that kind of exposure before. I only wish I had done this sooner.

錄音翻譯

問題 71~73 參照以下獨白。

當我把我的履歷貼上網站時，我並不確定那真的會帶來任何工作機會。我的意思是，我已經在用網路搜尋工作了，但是其實我認為最好的策略是尋找職缺，然後用電子郵件把履歷寄到人力資源處之類的。可是因為我的運氣不怎麼樣，於是我決定把履歷貼到幾個求職網站上。嗯，我告訴你怎麼回事。我在星期一把我的資料貼上去，到了星期三我就已經接到了徵才業者的電話。以前我要花好幾個星期才能得到這種曝光度，我真希望我早些這麼做。

題目&選項翻譯

71. 這名男子說他把履歷貼在哪裡？
    (A) 他的個人網站上
    (B) 幾個求職網站上
    (C) 最大的求職網站上
    (D) 某個大公司的網站上

72. 這名男子在把履歷貼上網前做了什麼？
    (A) 參加一些求才博覽會
    (B) 和幾家求才業者合作
    (C) 用電子郵件回覆求才公告
    (D) 靠報紙來找工作

73. 這名男子表示，把履歷貼上網的結果是什麼？
    (A) 他收到了更多不請自來的電子郵件。
    (B) 有求才業者找他。
    (C) 他在兩天內就找到了工作。
    (D) 他找到了更優質的工作機會。

☐ post [post] *v.* 張貼	☐ major corporation 大企業
☐ lead to 導致	☐ job fair 求才博覽會
☐ job offer 工作機會	☐ job posting 求才公告
☐ strategy [ˋstrætədʒɪ] *n.* 策略	☐ indicate [ˋɪndəˏket] *v.* 指出
☐ job opening [ˋopənɪŋ] 職缺	☐ unwanted [ʌnˋwɑntɪd] *adj.* 不要的
☐ recruiter [rɪˋkrutə] *n.* 招聘人員	☐ contact [ˋkɑntækt] *v.* 接觸
☐ exposure [ɪkˋspoʒə] *n.* 曝光	☐ job prospect [ˋprɑspɛkt] 工作機會

Questions 74~76　　　　　　　　　　　　　澳

74. 答案：(C)

破題 What/woman/say/company recent performance ⇨ 聽女子講公司近況。

解析 第一行 Overall, our products... 有介紹產品整體狀況的意思，因此後面的 ... well, <u>but</u> we lost a couple of clients last years. 即為其公司近來表現的狀況，故本題應選 (C)。

75. 答案：(D)

破題 What/woman/say/company/need/do ⇨ 聽取女子說公司要去做的「動作」字眼。

解析 由第四行 ... <u>we</u> <u>need</u> <u>to</u> <u>start</u> <u>producing</u> some <u>styles</u> at <u>lower</u> <u>prices</u> 及第八行 But I think the <u>future</u>... company is to move with the market... <u>start</u> <u>examining</u> how we can <u>extend</u> our <u>styles</u> to broaden our market <u>appeal</u>. 可看出，不論是 <u>lower</u> <u>prices</u> 或是 <u>extend</u> <u>styles</u>，目的皆在吸引不同的客戶，故應選 (D)。

76. 答案：(D)

破題 What/woman/imply/company ⇨ 聽女子說公司的「特質」。

解析 由第五行 I'm a little <u>concerned</u> about the <u>brand</u> <u>image</u> we've worked... to <u>establish</u>... a <u>line</u> of <u>inexpensive</u>, casual bags <u>doesn't</u> seem to <u>fit</u>... <u>consumers</u> have of our products. 可知，本題應選 (D)。

〔錄音內容〕
Questions 74 through 76 refer to the following talk.

Overall, our products are selling well, but we lost a couple of clients last year because we weren't hitting their price points—their customers were demanding lower quality, less expensive bags, and that's not something we do. If we want to stay competitive, we need to start producing some styles at lower prices. I'm a little concerned about the brand image we've worked so hard to establish over the past twenty years—a line of inexpensive, casual bags doesn't seem to fit with the perception most consumers have of our products. But I think the future of our company is to move with the market, and

I recommend we start examining how we can extend our styles to broaden our market appeal.

（錄音翻譯）

問題 74~76 參照以下獨白。

整體來說，我們的產品賣得很好，不過我們去年失去了幾個客戶，因為我們無法滿足他們要求的價位。他們的顧客要的是品質較低、價錢較便宜的包包，而我們所做的東西並非如此。假如我們想要保有競爭力，我們就要開始生產一些較低廉的款式。我有點擔心過去二十年來我們花這麼多工夫所建立起來的品牌形象，因為一系列廉價的休閒包似乎不符合大部分消費者對我們產品的觀感。不過我認為，我們公司將來勢必要隨著市場做調整。我建議我們應該開始審視，看看該如何延伸我們的款式，以提高我們的市場吸引力。

（題目＆選項翻譯）

74. 對於她們公司近來的表現，這名女子說了什麼？
    (A) 它的利潤大幅滑落。
    (B) 它的產品賣得不太好。
    (C) 它最近失去了幾個固定客戶。
    (D) 它必須將某些款式減產。

75. 這名女子說她們公司需要做什麼？
    (A) 開發新的品牌識別
    (B) 更貼近基本客戶
    (C) 生產更多高品質的產品
    (D) 吸引範圍更廣的顧客

76. 對於她們公司，這名女子暗示了什麼？
    (A) 它賣各式各樣廉價的產品。
    (B) 它的重點在於長期而非短期目標。
    (C) 它的形象因為銷售量下滑而受損。
    (D) 它是享譽盛名的高品質產品製造商。

- overall [ˌovəˋɔl] *adv.* 就整體來說
- hit [hɪt] *v.* 達到；擊中
- competitive [kəmˋpɛtətɪv] *adj.* 有競爭力的
- establish [əˋstæblɪʃ] *v.* 建立
- line [laɪn] *n.* （產品）系列
- inexpensive [ˌɪnɪkˋspɛnsɪv] *adj.* 價格低廉的
- casual [ˋkæʒuəl] *adj.* 休閒的；非正式的
- fit with 與……相稱
- perception [pɚˋsɛpʃən] *n.* 觀感；感受
- extend [ɪksˋtɛnd] *v.* 延伸
- broaden [ˋbrɔdn̩] *v.* 擴大
- appeal [əˋpil] *n.* 吸引力
- cut back 削減
- brand identity [aɪˋdɛntətɪ] 品牌識別
- a variety [vəˋraɪətɪ] of 各種的
- focus [ˋfokəs] *n.* （注意或活動等的）重點
- reputation [ˌrɛpjəˋteʃən] *n.* 信譽；名聲

Test 1
Part 1
Part 2
Part 3
Part 4
Test 2
Part 1
Part 2
Part 3
Part 4
簡
答

Questions 77~79

英

77. 答案：(C)

破題 How/man/plan/travel ⇨ 聽取男子說關於 travel 的「方式」。

解析 由 第 一 行 ... and I are going to be <u>spending</u> about a <u>week</u> <u>riding</u> our <u>bikes</u> down the western side of the state. 可知，其旅遊的方法為 (C) by bicycle。

78. 答案：(D)

破題 What/man/claim/C&O Canal ⇨ 聽取男子對運河的「看法或特色」。

解析 第三～五行都提到 C and O Canal，因此接下來第四行中的 it 即指該 Canal，後面即說明它的特色 ... that are <u>considered</u> some of the <u>earliest</u> pieces of <u>civil</u> <u>engineering</u> in <u>United</u> <u>States</u>.，故本題應選 (D)。

79. 答案：(A)

破題 What/man/imply/himself ⇨ 聽取男子說有關「自己」的字眼。

解析 第八行的 So aside from...（除了……之外）後面通常會有其他更重要的 資訊，因此其後的 there's a ton of history to learn about the explore —perfect for a history <u>buff</u> <u>like</u> me. 即為與本題有關的重點，故本題應選 (A)。

錄音內容

Questions 77 through 79 refer to the following talk.

Louise and I are going to be spending about a week riding our bikes down the western side of the state. We found a great bicycle trail that follows the C and O Canal for most of the way. The canal itself has a fascinating history. It has these aqueducts that were constructed in the nineteenth century, that are considered some of the earliest pieces of civil engineering in the United States. As a matter of fact, civil engineers generally mark the beginning of American civil engineering, as a field, to the construction of those aqueducts. So aside from being scenic trail, there's a ton of history to learn about and explore—perfect for a history buff like me.

Test 1

Part 1

Part 2

Part 3

Part 4

Test 2

Part 1

Part 2

Part 3

Part 4

簡

答

録音翻譯

問題 77~79 參照以下獨白。

我和露易絲要花一星期左右的時間到本州的西部做一趟單車之旅。我們發現了一條很棒的自行車道，沿途大部分都是繞行 C&O 運河。這條運河本身有很精彩的歷史。它擁有數條建於十九世紀的溝渠，這些溝渠並被認為是美國最早的一些土木工程。事實上，土木工程師普遍把這些溝渠的建造視為美國土木工程這個領域的起始點。所以那兒除了是條風景秀麗的自行車道外，還有一大堆歷史可供學習、探索。對像我這樣的歷史迷來說，這再完美不過了。

題目&選項翻譯

77. 這名男子打算如何旅行？
  (A) 開車
  (B) 搭船
  (C) 騎自行車
  (D) 搭觀光巴士

78. 針對 C&O 運河，這名男子提出了什麼看法？
  (A) 它幾乎蓋了一個世紀。
  (B) 它是由非美籍的工程師所設計的。
  (C) 它完成於十八世紀。
  (D) 它標示了美國木土工程的誕生。

79. 這名男子暗示了自己如何？
  (A) 他是業餘歷史學家。
  (B) 他擁有工程學位。
  (C) 他是在大學教歷史的教授。
  (D) 他寫了一本跟 C&O 運河有關的書。

□ bicycle trail 單車步道
□ canal [kə`næl] *n.* 運河
□ fascinating [`fæsn̩.etɪŋ] *adj.* 迷人的
□ aqueduct [`ækwɪ.dʌkt] *n.* 溝渠
□ construct [kən`strʌkt] *v.* 建造
□ civil engineering 土木工程
□ as a matter of fact 事實上 (= in fact)
□ aside from 除此之外

□ scenic [`sinɪk] *adj.* 景色秀麗的
□ a ton of 一大堆的
□ buff [bʌf] *n.*【美口】迷；愛好者
□ tour bus 觀光巴士
□ amateur [`æmətʃur] *n.*（科學、藝術、運動等的）業餘從事者
□ historian [hɪs`torɪən] *n.* 歷史學家
□ degree [dɪ`gri] *n.* 學位

 **Questions 80~82** 加

80. 答案：(D)

破題 What/subject/woman's talk ⇨ 聽女子講「主題、主旨」。以聽取前三行中的「名詞」為主。

解析 由第一行 Maybe you've heard the phrase "<u>Form</u>, <u>Storm</u>, <u>Norm</u>, <u>Perform</u> ... <u>but</u> I <u>think</u> <u>it</u> <u>describes</u> a real <u>process</u>... <u>project team</u>... <u>go through</u>. 可知，本題應選 (D)。

81. 答案：(D)

破題 What/woman/claim/cause/misunderstanding/team ⇨ 聽取女子說「因果」字眼的「因」。

解析 要注意本題考造成「果」之「因」。說話者先在第三行先提到「因」：... several individuals on the team who've <u>never</u> <u>worked</u> <u>together</u>...，之後則提到「果」：<u>initially</u>, <u>some misunderstanding</u> <u>occur</u>，故應選 (D)。

82. 答案：(B)

破題 woman/what happens/after/disagreements ⇨ 聽女子說 disagreements 發生的相關句子。

解析 在第四句 maybe some <u>disagreement</u>... or <u>misunderstanding</u>... 之後聽到 But...，後面即是解決方案：... <u>eventually</u> the team figures out a way to work together，故本題應選 (B)。

录音內容

Questions 80 through 82 refer to the following talk.

Maybe you've heard the phrase, "Form, Storm, Norm, Perform." It's funny, I know, but I think it describes a real process that project teams all go through. First, the team is formed—there are probably several individuals on the team who've never worked together, and it's natural that, initially, some misunderstandings occur. So the team goes through a little storm—maybe some disagreement about creative decisions, or misunderstanding around project roles. But whatever the reason, eventually the team figures out a way to work together, it develops its norms—people settle into however they feel

Test 1

Part 1

Part 2

Part 3

Part 4

Test 2

Part 1

Part 2

Part 3

Part 4

about each other and learn to anticipate problems and work around them. And that's when the team really starts to perform.

（錄音翻譯）
問題 80~82 參照以下獨白。

也許你聽過這句話：「形成、激盪、規範、執行」。我知道它很好笑，不過我想它描述了專案團隊都必須經歷的實際過程。首先是團隊的組成——團隊裡大概會有好幾個從來沒有共事過的人，所以一開始自然會有一些誤解產生。於是團隊就會經歷一點激盪——也許是一些關於做出創意決策的爭論，或是關於專案中角色的誤解。但不管原因為何，團隊終究會找到共事的方法，發展出它的規範——成員們會習慣對彼此的感覺並學著預測問題並加以解決。而這也是團隊真正開始執行的時候。

（題目&選項翻譯）
80. 這名女子所談的主題是什麼？
　　(A) 組成專案團隊的最佳方式
　　(B) 她最近參加的一個專案團隊
　　(C) 她最近所觀察到的績效問題
　　(D) 專案團隊通常會經歷的階段

81. 這名女子表示什麼事可能會在團隊中引起誤解？
　　(A) 有關錢的問題之爭論
　　(B) 團隊成員之間的競爭
　　(C) 缺乏一套明確的期望
　　(D) 團隊成員對彼此不熟悉

82. 依照這名女子的說法，當專案團隊中的人出現爭論後，通常會發生什麼事？
　　(A) 他們的工作表現會下滑。
　　(B) 他們會發展出自然的工作慣例。
　　(C) 他們會變得更難管理。
　　(D) 他們會排斥一起參與未來的專案。

- ☐ phrase [frez] *n.* 用語
- ☐ storm [stɔrm] *n.* 風暴;大動盪
- ☐ norm [nɔrm] *n.* 規範
- ☐ go through 經歷
- ☐ individual [ˌɪndə`vɪdʒuəl] *n.* 個人
- ☐ initially [ɪ`nɪʃəlɪ] *adv.* 起初
- ☐ misunderstanding [ˌmɪsʌndə`stændɪŋ] *n.* 誤解
- ☐ disagreement [ˌdɪsə`grimənt] *n.* 意見不一

- ☐ creative [kri`etɪv] *adj.* 有創造力的
- ☐ eventually [ɪ`vɛntʃuəlɪ] *adv.* 最終
- ☐ figure out 想出
- ☐ settle [`sɛtl] *v.* 解決(問題)
- ☐ anticipate [æn`tɪsəˌpet] *v.* 預期
- ☐ observe [əb`zɝv] *v.* 觀察
- ☐ phase [fez] *n.* 階段
- ☐ routine [ru`tin] *n.* 慣例;日常事務
- ☐ resist [rɪ`zɪst] *v.* 抗拒

Test 1

Part
1

Part
2

Part
3

Part
4

Test 2

Part
1

Part
2

Part
3

Part
4

簡

答

MP3 185 Questions 83~85 英

83. 答案：(D)

破 題 What/can/inferred ⇨ 根據已知的線索或訊息來推斷。

解 析 第一行 You <u>attention</u> please. 後面即為重點：This is the <u>last announcement</u> before...，由 the last announcement 可知之前已有其他通告，故應選 (D)。

84. 答案：(B)

破 題 What/going/happen/during/test/PTV system ⇨ 聽取那段時間內的「動作」相關字眼。

解 析 由第三行 During the test, ... the <u>system's</u> <u>pressure</u> will be <u>raised</u> to a maximum... 可知，本題應選 (B)。

85. 答案：(B)

破 題 What/announcement/ask/people/do ⇨ 聽取「命令」、「要求」或「建議」等字眼。

解 析 本題有二次線索可得知答案。由第五行 Because the potential risk is higher than normal, the entire building <u>needs</u> to be <u>evacuated</u>，以及第八行 <u>Again</u>, please evacuate the building immediately. 可知，正確答案為 (B)。

錄音內容

Questions 83 through 85 refer to the following announcement.

Your attention please. This is the last announcement before the test of the P-T-V system. For the next ninety minutes, the Oceanography department will be conducting a routine test of the particle tracking velocimetry system. During the test, the system's pressure will be raised to a maximum of ten-thousand P-S-I. Because the potential risk is higher than normal, the entire building needs to be evacuated. You will need to remain away from the building for the full ninety minutes. An all-clear announcement will be made to alert you when it is safe to re-enter the building. Again, please evacuate the building immediately. This is the last announcement before the test begins. Thank you.

录音翻譯

問題 83~85 參照以下通告。

各位請注意。這是 PTV 系統測試前的最後一次通告。在接下來的九十分鐘內，海洋部將對分子移動測速系統展開例行測試。在測試期間，系統壓力將調高到最大的一萬 PSI。由於潛在風險比平常來得高，因此整棟大樓需要淨空。在這整整九十分鐘裡，各位要跟大樓保持距離。當大家可以安全地重返大樓時，會有警報解除通告來提醒各位。再說一次，請立刻淨空大樓。這是測試開始前的最後一次通告，謝謝。

题目&選項翻譯

83. 對於此通告我們可做什麼樣的推論？
    (A) 它每週都在同一時間發布。
    (B) 它是以幾棟大樓裡的人為對象。
    (C) 它由部門主管直接下達。
    (D) 它是接在稍早所發布過的其他通告後面。

84. 在 PTV 系統測試期間會發生什麼事？
    (A) 整個系統會停止運轉。
    (B) 該系統的壓力會提高。
    (C) 有毒化學物質可能會從系統中冒出來。
    (D) 熱度可能會升高到令人不適的程度。

85. 此通告要大家做什麼？
    (A) 注意可能的危險
    (B) 立刻離開大樓
    (C) 關閉所有的電腦設備
    (D) 寫下所看到的一切

- announcement [əˋnaʊnsmənt] n. 通告
- particle [ˋpɑrtɪkl] n. 【物】粒子；質點
- oceanography [oʃɪəˋnɑgrəfɪ] n. 海洋學
- conduct [kənˋdʌkt] v. 實施
- routine [ruˋtin] adj. 例行的
- velocimetry [ˌvɛləˋsɪmətrɪ] n. 測速
- maximum [ˋmæksəməm] n. 最大量；最大限
- potential [pəˋtɛnʃəl] adj. 潛在的；可能的
- evacuate [ɪˋvækjʊˌet] v. 撤離
- all-clear [ˋɔlˋklɪr] adj. 空襲警報解除的
- alert [əˋlɜt] v. 向……發布警報
- immediately [ɪˋmidɪɪtlɪ] adv. 立刻
- shut down 停工
- toxic [ˋtɑksɪk] adj. 有毒的
- chemical [ˋkɛmɪkl] n. 化學製品 adj. 化學的
- emerge [ɪˋmɜdʒ] v. 浮現
- hazard [ˋhæzəd] n. 危險（物）
- shut off 關掉

 **Questions 86~88**　　　　　　　　　　　　　加

86. 答案：(C)

破 題 How long/repair garage/privatized ⇨ 聽取修車行 privatized 的「時間長度」。

解 析 由第一行 In its <u>first</u> <u>year</u> of operation, ... <u>privatized</u> city repair garage... 可知，本題應選 (C)。

87. 答案：(B)

破 題 What/resulted from/privatization ⇨ 聽取「結果」的「果」。

解 析 第六行 According to..., 為表事實的句型，後面接著的 ... rather than saving money, the city is <u>actually</u> going to end up <u>spending</u> <u>five hundred thousand</u> dollars more on <u>vehicle repair</u>. 即為答案，故應選 (B)。

88. 答案：(D)

破 題 What/not mentioned/vehicles/serviced by/city repair garage ⇨ 聽取獨白中「密集性排列」名詞中沒提到的單位名稱。

解 析 由第三行 <u>The repair garage</u>, which services vehicles belonging to the police, fire, sanitation... 可知，正確答案為 (D)。

〔錄音內容〕

Questions 86 through 88 refer to the following news report.

In its first year of operation, Louisville's privatized city repair garage has failed to save the city money, according to an audit released today by city controller Richard Weeks. The repair garage, which services city vehicles belonging to the police, fire, sanitation, and other departments, was touted as likely to save the city one-point-five million dollars when it was privatized last year. According to the city controller's audit, rather than saving money, the city is actually going to end up spending almost five hundred thousand dollars more on vehicle repair. Vehicle Best, the contractor who took over the garage, did not respond to the controller's report.

125

(錄音翻譯)

問題 86~88 參照以下新聞報導。

根據市府主計長理查‧威克斯今天所公布的決算，在營運的頭一年，路易斯維爾的民營市立修車行並沒有幫市府省到錢。該修車行負責維修警局、消防隊、衛生局及其他部門的市屬車輛，去年改為民營時，號稱可以為市府省下一百五十萬美元。但是根據市府主計長的決算，市府不但沒有省錢，最後反而要多花將近五十萬美元在修車上。對於主計長的報告，接手的包商「最優車行」並沒有做出回應。

(題目&選項翻譯)

86. 修車行民營化了多久？
    (A) 幾週
    (B) 五個月
    (C) 一年
    (D) 五年

87. 根據這份報告，將市立修車行民營化造成了什麼結果？
    (A) 市府省下了一百五十萬美元。
    (B) 市府多花了五十萬美元。
    (C) 市府有更多的車輛停擺。
    (D) 市府受到聯邦政府稽查。

88. 文中「沒有」提到哪個市府部門把車交給市立修車行維修？
    (A) 消防局
    (B) 警局
    (C) 衛生局
    (D) 監理所

□ operation [ˌɑpəˋreʃən] *n.* 運作
□ privatize [ˋpraɪvəˌtaɪz] *v.* 使民營化
□ audit [ˋɔdɪt] *n.* 稽核
□ release [rɪˋlis] *v.* 發佈（新聞稿等）
□ controller [kənˋtrolə] *n.* 主計長
□ sanitation [ˌsænəˋteʃən] *n.*（公共）衛生
□ tout [taʊt] 極力推薦

□ end up + V-ing 以……收場
□ contractor [ˋkɑntræktə] *n.* 承包商
□ take over 接管
□ extra [ˋɛkstrə] *adj.* 額外的；外加的
□ federal government 聯邦政府
□ motor vehicle department 監理所

Test 1

Part 1

Part 2

Part 3

Part 4

Test 2

Part 1

Part 2

Part 3

Part 4

簡

答

Questions 89~91

澳

89. 答案：(C)

破　題 Why/Carolyn River/called ⇨ 問「主旨」，通常在打電話的一開始就會提到。

解　析 由第一行 Hello, Mr. O'Toole... my name... Carolyn Rivers... 和第二行 Your <u>name</u> was <u>recommended</u> to us by... of the... Country club. 可知，正確答案為 (C)。

90. 答案：(B)

破　題 What/Carolyn/want/do ⇨ 聽取「動作」字眼。

解　析 第四行 I'm calling to let you know... and would love to <u>meet</u> with <u>you</u> to <u>discuss</u>... products... <u>business</u>. 可知，本題應選 (B)。

91. 答案：(A)

破　題 What/can/inferred/Mr. O'Toole ⇨ 聽取女子提與 Mr. O'Toole 相關的線索來推論。

解　析 由第四行的 I'm calling tot let you know I'll be in Boston next week...，可推知答案為 (A)。

（錄音內容）

Questions 89 through 91 refer to the following voicemail message.

Hello Mr. O'Toole, my name is Carolyn Rivers and I'm with High Performance Sporting Goods. Your name was recommended to us by Juan Gonzalez of the Fairways Country Club. Juan indicated you may be interested in the line of products we carry, particularly our new Golflite golf bag. I'm calling to let you know I'll be in Boston next week, and would love to meet with you to discuss how our products might be able to help your business. I'll try to reach you again to make an appointment—in the meantime, you can call me at one-eight-hundred, four-one-two, one-two-five-oh. I'm also taking the liberty of sending you our current catalog. Thank you, and I very much look forward to speaking with you.

録音翻譯

問題 89~91 參照以下語音郵件訊息。

哈囉，奧圖先生，我是「高效能運動用品」的卡洛琳‧里弗斯。您的大名承蒙「球道鄉村俱樂部」的璜‧岡薩雷斯推薦給我們。璜說您可能會對我們所販售的系列產品感興趣，尤其是我們新的「輕穎」高球袋。我打電話來是要讓您知道，我下星期會到波士頓並且很樂意去拜訪您，以討論我們的產品對您的事業可以有什麼幫助。我會試著再次聯絡您以約定會面時間，同時您也可以打這支電話給我：1800-412-1250。恕我冒昧地把我們現有的目錄寄給您。感謝您，十分期待跟您面談。

題目&選項翻譯

89. 卡洛琳‧里弗斯為什麼要打電話給奧圖先生？
   (A) 她之前告訴他說她會打電話。
   (B) 他留了語音訊息要她回電。
   (C) 有同僚把他的名字給她。
   (D) 他之前向她們公司訂了目錄。

90. 卡洛琳‧里弗斯想要做什麼？
   (A) 確認訂單
   (B) 安排會面
   (C) 重訂送貨時間
   (D) 提供貸款額度

91. 對於奧圖先生我們可以做什麼樣的推論？
   (A) 他在波士頓附近工作。
   (B) 他開了一家鄉村俱樂部。
   (C) 他是職業高爾夫選手。
   (D) 他目前在販售里弗斯女士的某一系列產品。

- □ indicate [ˈɪndə‚ket] v. 指出
- □ carry [ˈkærɪ] v. 有……出售
- □ reach [rɪtʃ] v. 與……取得聯繫
- □ make an appointment 約定會面時間
- □ take the liberty of... 冒昧地做……
- □ current [ˈkɝənt] adj. 當前的；現行的
- □ voicemail [ˈvɔɪs‚mel] n. 語音訊息
- □ colleague [ˈkɑlig] n. 同事
- □ previously [ˈprivɪəslɪ] adv. 以前
- □ line of credit 信用貸款額度
- □ golfer [ˈgolfə] n. 打高爾夫球的人

Questions 92~94
英

92. 答案：(B)

破題 What/information/salt/not provide ⇨ 聽取與鹽相關的訊息。

解析 本題為「密集式排列敘述」題型。由第一行中提到的 Excess salt consumption，一直到第四行中的 ... average adult should eat less than... salt per day 皆為此題的敘述，而答案 (B) The total quantity consumed worldwide 並不在其中，故為正確答案。

93. 答案：(A)

破題 What/speaker/claim/salt consumption/US ⇨ 聽取與 salt consumption 有關訊息。

解析 第五行 Yet, on average, Americans consume more than thirty-three hundred... up from thirty-one hundred ten years ago. 可知，故本題應選 (A)。注意，本句中的 up 表「增加」的概念，這類包含表「不同、改變」字眼的句子，常為出題重點。

94. 答案：(D)

破題 What/speaker/suggest/happen ⇨ 聽取「說話者」表建議的「動作性」字眼。

解析 第九行 Which is why we need to pressure the food industry to try to get them to cut down on salt. 中的 why... need to 句型用來表「建議」，後面的敘述即為答案，故本題應選 (D)。

(錄音內容)
Questions 92 through 94 refer to the following talk.

Excess salt consumption is linked certainly to heart disease, and possibly to several other health problems. Part of the reason this is a concern to us is that salt consumption in the U.S. is at an all-time high. Government dietary guidelines tell us that the average adult should eat less than twenty-three hundred milligrams of salt per day. Yet, on average, Americans consume more than thirty-three hundred milligrams—and this is up from thirty-one hundred ten years ago. The problem is, about three-quarters of this comes from processed food. Only about ten percent is contained naturally in foods, and maybe another ten comes out of the salt shaker. Which is why we need to pressure the food industry to try to get them to cut down on salt.

(錄音翻譯)
問題 92~94 參照以下獨白。

鹽吃得太多顯然跟心臟病有關，跟其他好幾種健康問題可能也有關聯。我們之所以關心這點有部分原因是，在美國鹽的消耗量達到了歷年來的新高。政府的飲食準則告訴我們，一般成人每天不應攝取超過兩千三百毫克的鹽。然而，平均來說，美國人所吃下的鹽卻超過了三千三百毫克，而且是從十年前的三千一百毫克逐步增加。問題在於，這其中大約有三分之二是來自加工食品，只有大約十分之一自然包含在食物中，另外還有十分之一也許來自鹽罐。這就是為什麼我們要對食品業施壓，以設法讓他們減少用鹽量。

(題目&選項翻譯)
92. 說話者「沒有」提到哪一項與鹽相關的訊息？
　　(A) 每個人的總消耗量
　　(B) 全世界的總消耗量
　　(C) 建議的攝取鹽量
　　(D) 鹽和健康問題的可能關係

93. 關於美國鹽的消耗說話者說了什麼？
　　(A) 它過去十年有所增加。
　　(B) 它是應有分量的兩倍之多。
　　(C) 它造成了國內健康成本提高。
　　(D) 它高過其他任何一個工業化國家。

94. 說話者建議應該做什麼？
　　(A) 政府應該訂定新的準則。
　　(B) 應該進行更多的醫學研究。
　　(C) 大家應該在食物裡少放鹽。
　　(D) 食品業應該在食物裡少放鹽。

- excess [ɪkˋsɛs] *adj.* 過量的
- consumption [kənˋsʌmpʃən] *n.* 消耗
- be linked to 與⋯⋯有關
- heart disease 心臟病
- dietary [ˋdaɪəˌtɛrɪ] *adj.* 飲食的
- on average [ˋævərɪdʒ] 平均上
- consume [kənˋsjum] *v.* 消耗
- processed [ˋprɑsɛst] food 加工過的食物

- salt shaker [ˋsɔlt ˌʃekɚ]【美】鹽罐
- industry [ˋɪndəstrɪ] *n.* 產業
- cut down 削減
- quantity [ˋkwɑntətɪ] *n.* 量
- worldwide [ˋwɝldˋwaɪd] *adv.* 在全世界
- industrialized [ɪnˋdʌstrɪəlˌaɪzd] *adj.* 工業化的

Test 1
Part 1
Part 2
Part 3
Part 4
Test 2
Part 1
Part 2
Part 3
Part 4
簡答

MP3 189 **Questions 95~97** 加

95. 答案：(C)

破 題 Who/woman/talk about ⇨ 聽女子講另一人的「名字」、「職稱」或「和兩人關係」。

解 析 由第二、三行 We're both... grown up together. ... most rewarding <u>business relationships</u> I've ever had. 可知，答案為 (C)。

96. 答案：(B)

破 題 What/field/woman/work ⇨ 聽取女子提「工作性質」之字眼。

解 析 由第一行 I met Ross soon after I began <u>designing</u> <u>interiors</u>. 以及第四行中的 ... learned to <u>design</u> my <u>interiors</u>... 可知，本題應選 (B)。

97. 答案：(A)

破 題 What/woman/claim/Ross ⇨ 聽取女子對 Ross 的敘述。

解 析 由第八行 And now <u>he</u> has a large staff... 可知，本題應選 (A)。

[錄音內容]

Questions 95 through 97 refer to the following talk.

I met Ross soon after I began designing interiors. At the time, we were both starting our careers, and, well, over the years, we've both sort of grown up together. It's one of the most rewarding business relationships I've ever had—any kind of furniture I can design, he can construct, and in turn, I've learned to design my interiors around his strengths. He does everything for our firm, from stand-alone custom furniture pieces to entire libraries, kitchens, staircases, you name it—it's not unusual for his work to fill an entire one of my houses. And now he has a large staff and so do I, and we don't always get to work directly with each other. But when we do, it's like old times.

Test 1

Part

1

Part

2

Part

3

Part

4

Test 2

Part

1

Part

2

Part

3

Part

4

簡

答

録音翻譯

問題 95~97 參照以下獨白。

在我開始從事室內設計後沒多久，就認識了羅斯。當時我們都在開創自己的職涯，而這些年來，我們倆也算是一起成長。這是我所遇過最有益於事業的關係之一——只要我能設計出任何一種家具，他就能做得出來，而後來我便學會了依他的強項來做室內設計。我們公司的一切都是他做的，從獨立的特製家具到整個圖書室、廚房、樓梯間，只要你說得出來，他就做的出來——他的作品塞滿我設計的房子是常有的事。現在他擁有陣容龐大的員工，而我也是。我們並非總是直接跟對方合作，但是當我們這麼做時，就彷彿回到了過去。

題目&選項翻譯

95. 這名女子在講的人是誰？
(A) 客戶
(B) 員工
(C) 事業夥伴
(D) 大學時的朋友

96. 這名女子很可能是在哪個領域工作？
(A) 家具銷售
(B) 室內設計
(C) 住宅營造
(D) 家具製造

97. 這名女子提到了羅斯的什麼事？
(A) 他有很多員工。
(B) 他是個老年人。
(C) 他過去在圖書館工作。
(D) 他完全靠手工在做家具。

□ interior [ɪn`tɪrɪə] *n.* 內部
□ sort of 有幾分
□ career [kə`rɪr] *n.* 職業生涯
□ rewarding [rɪ`wɔrdɪŋ] *adj.* 有益的
□ in turn 反之
□ strength [strɛŋθ] *n.* 強項

□ stand-alone [`stændəlon] *adj.* 獨力的；單獨的
□ custom furniture 特製家具
□ staircase [`stɛr.kes] *n.* 樓梯間
□ you name it 你列舉出來
□ senior citizen 老年人

133

Questions 98~100

美

98. 答案：(A)

破題 What/advice/man/give/first/began/career ⇨ 聽取與 began his career 相關的建議。

解析 第二句中出現與題目有關的字眼：When I started my first job...，後面的敘述部分 I was <u>told</u> to be five minutes early, to look <u>professional</u>... 即包含了答案，故本題應選 (A)。

99. 答案：(B)

破題 What/man's job ⇨ 聽取男子提「工作」或「職業」的名稱。

解析 由第五行 But more important for <u>managers</u> is how <u>we</u> prepare for meetings. 和第六行 I always... before every meeting... 可推知，他擔任的工作為 (B)。

100. 答案：(D)

破題 What/man/not/clam/do/before/meeting ⇨ 聽取男子說有關會前的「動作」字眼。

解析 本題考「密集性排列敘述」，要一邊聽一邊去確認選項。由第六行 I <u>always</u> spend a few minutes before every meeting <u>looking over</u> my <u>notes</u>, <u>writing down questions</u>, <u>looking over</u> the <u>agenda</u>... 的敘述可知，(D) Note who is running the meeting 並未被提及，故為正確答案。

錄音內容

Questions 98 through 100 refer to the following talk.

Managers have to be aware of the impression they make in meetings—whether it's an internal meeting or a business presentation for a new client. When I started my first job in the corporate world, I was told to be five minutes early, to look professional and carry my papers in a professional binder. These little gestures mean a lot! But more important for managers is how we prepare for meetings. I always spend a few minutes before every meeting looking over my notes, writing down questions, looking over the agenda, and becoming prepared for the entire scope of the meeting, whether or not I'm running it. If everybody goes into the meeting prepared, work gets done!

Test 1
Part 1
Part 2
Part 3
Part 4
Test 2
Part 1
Part 2
Part 3
Part 4

錄音翻譯

問題 98~100 參照以下獨白。

經理人必須了解自己在開會時——不論是內部會議還是向新客戶提出業務報告——給人的印象。我開始在企業界做第一份工作時，就被告知必須提早五分鐘到、要看起來專業，而且把書面資料放在專業的夾子裡。這些小動作可是大有學問！但是對經理人來說，更重要的是要如何做好會議的準備。在每次開會之前，我都會花幾分鐘複習我的筆記、寫下問題、檢視議程，以便為整場會議做好準備，不管那場會議是不是由我主持。假如每一個人都能做好準備再去開會，自然可以功成圓滿！

題目&選項翻譯

98. 當這名男子第一次展開職業生涯時，他得到了什麼建議？
 (A) 一定要看起來專業
 (B) 一定要帶名片
 (C) 要參加專業會議
 (D) 要學習如何提出報告

99. 這名男子可能擔任什麼工作？
 (A) 公司訓練人員
 (B) 公司經理
 (C) 企業顧問
 (D) 業務代表

100. 這名男子「沒有」提到在每次業務會議前要做什麼？
 (A) 複習筆記
 (B) 寫下問題
 (C) 檢視開會議程
 (D) 注意會議由誰主持

□ be aware of 意識到
□ impression [ɪmˋprɛʃən] *n.* 印象
□ internal [ɪnˋtɝnl] *adj.* 內部的
□ presentation [ˌprɛznˋteʃən] *n.* 簡報
□ binder [ˋbaɪndɚ] *n.* 夾子
□ look over 仔細檢查
□ scope [skop] *n.* 範圍；領域
□ business card 名片
□ consultant [kənˋsʌltənt] *n.* 顧問
□ sales representative 業務代表
□ examine [ɪgˋzæmɪn] *v.* 檢查

模擬試題
簡答

Test 1

Part 1

No.	ANSWER	No.	ANSWER	No.	ANSWER	No.	ANSWER
1	C	11	A	21	A	31	D
2	D	12	B	22	D	32	D
3	A	13	A	23	A	33	A
4	B	14	C	24	C	34	D
5	A	15	A	25	D	35	B
6	A	16	C	26	A	36	C
7	B	17	A	27	B	37	B
8	C	18	A	28	B	38	B
9	A	19	C	29	A	39	C
10	D	20	A	30	C	40	C

Part 2 (No. 11–40) · **Part 3** (No. 41–70) · **Part 4** (No. 71–100)

No.	ANSWER	No.	ANSWER	No.	ANSWER
41	A	51	A	61	A
42	D	52	D	62	C
43	B	53	C	63	B
44	D	54	D	64	D
45	C	55	B	65	A
46	A	56	B	66	C
47	C	57	C	67	B
48	B	58	B	68	C
49	B	59	B	69	D
50	C	60	D	70	A

No.	ANSWER	No.	ANSWER	No.	ANSWER
71	A	81	A	91	A
72	B	82	B	92	D
73	D	83	A	93	B
74	A	84	C	94	B
75	B	85	D	95	C
76	C	86	B	96	D
77	D	87	A	97	C
78	C	88	C	98	B
79	D	89	A	99	D
80	C	90	D	100	A

Test 2

Part 1 (No. 1–10) · **Part 2** (No. 11–40) · **Part 3** (No. 41–70) · **Part 4** (No. 71–100)

Each question is answered on the ANSWER grid with columns A B C D.